Protecting the Movie Star

The Protectors: Book Four

SAMANTHA CHASE
NOELLE ADAMS

This book is a work of fiction. Names, characters, places, and incidents are the product of the authors' imaginations or are used fictitiously. Any resemblance to actual events, locales, or persons, living or dead, is coincidental.

Copyright © 2017 by Samantha Chase and Noelle Adams. All rights reserved, including the right to reproduce, distribute, or transmit in any form or by any means.

PROLOGUE
Cole

One of the clearest memories I have of my friend, Gavin, was just a normal day, an unimportant conversation. I'm not sure why the memory is burned into my brain.

The mail had just come.

When you're deployed, there are times you are anxious for anything from home—a care package or just something familiar, something to make you feel less like you're thousands of miles away. All the guys in my unit get stuff sent to them from home.

Not me.

There was no one back home missing me, and there was no one looking to make me feel better.

It didn't bother me. There were always guys in my unit who didn't mind sharing. On that day I remember, I looked around and spotted Gavin sitting and reading.

"Are you seriously reading *People Magazine?*" I asked, trying not to laugh.

Gavin flipped me the finger but didn't look up from the glossy pages he was obviously engrossed in. "Shh. I'm trying to decide who wore it better."

I yanked the magazine from his hands and grinned when he reached for it. "Maybe next time you should ask someone to send you Playboy, not People."

"Right. Because I'm going to ask my sister to send me porn." Gavin spoke in a deadpan, still reaching for the magazine but refusing to get up. "C'mon. I'm bored out of my mind here today. Let me just look at the pretty people and forget that I'm surrounded by your ugly faces."

Because I enjoyed annoying him, I took another step back and began looking through the pages of the magazine. "Geez, what a bunch of superficial assholes," I murmured. "The worst thing anyone in here has to worry about is if their outfit makes them look fat. They should try walking around the dessert with a hundred pounds of gear on their back."

With a sigh, Gavin put his arm down. "I'm not reading it because it's intellectually stimulating, you idiot. I'm reading it so, for a few damn minutes, I can think about something other than this place. It's mindless reading. Now give it back."

I flipped through a few more pages, and it just pissed me off. Pretty people posing for the camera without a care in the world.

Must be nice.

I was sitting here in sweltering temperatures and wondering if I was going to live to see tomorrow, and I was getting a crappy paycheck for it. These people were sitting in their mansions with others waiting on them hand and foot, and they were making millions just because they're beautiful. Talk about injustice.

I flung the magazine back at him with disgust.

"Personally, I'd rather read nothing than that crap."

"Don't be hating," Gavin said as he began reading again. "Ooh, a new Batman movie and a new 007! Nice!"

I couldn't help but roll my eyes.

"They'll be old news by the time we get to see them," I commented, taking a seat next to him on the ground.

Putting the magazine aside, Gavin looked at me with mild annoyance. "Could you maybe go for more than a minute without being a pessimistic pain in the ass? I'm trying to just relax here for a few minutes, and your constant negative comments are really getting on my nerves."

He was right. I was a pessimistic person, but that wasn't going to change any time soon. Especially not living in this nightmare. I'd escaped one nightmare and exchanged it for another.

Lucky me.

"So what's your deal? I mean, basically I know what your deal is, but why take it out on some stupid magazine? No one's asking you to read it," Gavin said.

"It's what it all represents. Wouldn't it be nice if we could make millions of dollars for memorizing a couple of lines of dialogue while someone does our hair and walks our dogs? It's bullshit, man."

"Yeah, okay, I get that. But again, no one's asking you to read it. Harper sends me different stuff every month to keep me entertained." He gave me a lopsided grin. "It's not like I have a subscription and I'm making you pay for half of it or something."

Again, he was right. I was just in a pissy mood.

Actually, I was always in a pissy mood.

I was here in Afghanistan and I wasn't sure when I was going home. Not that I had a home that I wanted to go back to. I grew up in shitty circumstances, and no matter how hard I tried to change them or escape, I couldn't seem to catch a break. And what was worse, these guys who were now my friends had no idea how lucky they have it.

I looked away from Gavin and toward the rest of the guys milling around. Everything was quiet right now, and the mail had finally gotten delivered about an hour ago.

Hence Gavin's magazine.

He elbowed me, and I turned back to him. "Harper also sent some cookies." He held up a tin to me, and there were a bunch of chocolate chip cookies in there. "Take some before anyone else sees them. I know for a fact Levi will try and horde them all if I tell him I have them."

Laughing quietly, I took a few. "Thanks, man. I appreciate it."

Gavin always shared the stuff he got from home. So did Levi. And Sebastian. No one ever came right out and mentioned that I never got anything, and for that I was grateful. I usually tried to find something to do when the mail truck came—no need to draw attention to the fact that nothing ever came for me.

"What else did you get?" I asked.

Twisting away, Gavin reached for the box and put it between us and began going through it. "The cookies, the magazine, some socks," he said with a laugh, "a toothbrush and some other toiletry crap that she insists I need and, huh, a letter." Taking it out of the box, Gavin opened the envelope and unfolded the paper from inside as he sat back to read it.

Lucky bastard.

The pang of envy hit me harder than it ever had before.

Getting a letter from someone who actually gave a damn if you were dead or alive must be nice.

Beside me, he let out a low laugh at something his sister had written.

Maybe I should have gone to sit someplace else. Suddenly it felt like I was invading his privacy by staying there, but when I looked around, it seemed like everyone was reading something from home.

With nothing else to do, I picked up the damn magazine and began flipping through the pages again.

Look at all the superficial pretty people.

Shit.

If I ever met one of these fuckers, I'd seriously have to punch them in the face.

~

A few years later, and not very much had changed. I'd come home. Gavin had died. I had friends when I'd never really had them before the Marines. But it still felt like things weren't right in my life.

And today was worse than normal.

I'd never been one to say no to a challenge, but right now as I stared up at the massive structure in front of me, I wasn't sure if I could do this. No one would even know. I could just drive away, and no one would be the wiser.

I don't want to do this.

There are things you have control over and those you don't. I should have been a pro at spotting the difference between the two. My life had been nothing but a never-ending list of shit I didn't want to do. Granted, I ended up doing most of them, but this? This was avoidable.

Utterly and completely avoidable.

I looked at the building and then at my keys and back again. No one knew I was here. Sure, it was pretty much expected, but then again, most people knew better than to expect anything from me. I played by my own rules now. For far too long I'd been forced to live by everyone else's rules, expectations, and demands. This was my time now.

The pep talk normally did it for me, and under any other circumstances, I might have already been a couple of miles away by now without giving it a second thought. But for some reason, I couldn't seem to make myself move.

You owe it to them.

Shit. Yes. No. Maybe. I shouldn't feel the need to owe anything to anybody. Not ever again. But there was that voice inside me telling me otherwise. I didn't like thinking about it—owing anyone—but in this instance, there was a pretty damn good chance that I did. It was the least I could do.

You owe it to me.

And that was it in a nutshell. It wasn't even my voice right now talking to me. It was his. Gavin's. Hell, I'd give everything I had to actually have him here beside me, talking to me, telling me to stop being a pussy and get my ass out of the car. He'd laugh at me, and I'd bitch about it, but in the end, I'd get up and go.

I slammed my head back against the headrest. All this time and it still got me by the throat. Suddenly my heart was racing and I was breaking out in a sweat. PTSD. I thought it was a load of BS when I first heard about it, but now that I'd experienced it—hell, I was experiencing it right now!—I knew it was real.

Deep breaths. In. Out. Repeat.

You can do this.

I had to get myself together. There was no other choice. I was not going to sit here in my damn car and let my anxiety—or anything else for that matter—get the better of me. I was stronger than that. I was getting better. Maybe if I said it enough, I'd actually start to believe it.

You can do this—for me.

"Dammit, Gavin," I muttered.

And that was all it took. Saying his name out loud was my own way of facing my demons. It was like a blast of cold water in the face. He wasn't there. He was never going to be there again.

Because of me.

I'd only cried once in my life. And it was that day. When I knew Gavin was gone and I was the reason for it, I cried until I couldn't breathe. I cried until my body ached. It was already bloodied and torn up from the explosion, but I didn't feel any of those injuries. No. What I felt, I felt in my heart as it tore in two.

I'd killed my best friend.

A loud knock on my window had me nearly jumping out of my skin. Quickly turning my head, it took a minute for me to get myself back in the present. As things came into focus, I saw Declan standing next to my car.

"Yo, are you ever getting out of the damn car?" he said with a chuckle. "I've been standing here for five minutes."

Well... shit. Totally missed that. "Yeah, yeah," I grumbled. "Keep your panties on." With no other choice, I grabbed my keys and climbed out.

It was hard to get anything by Declan, and I guess I was pretty transparent at the moment. "You okay?" he asked. "You look a little... off."

I swiped a hand over my face. "What? Yeah, no, I'm fine."

He stared at me for a minute and then turned and looked over his shoulder to the building behind us. "I hate going in there."

"Me too."

"I mean, we're here for a good thing, but... you know. Still."

I guess that was the good thing about being friends with people who had gone through what I had. Sometimes there wasn't a need for words. We just knew.

"I've been sitting out here for a while now," I finally said. "It's just a building. I know that. But sometimes it's just a sound... or a smell..."

"I know," Declan said somberly. "I pretty much talked to myself the whole way here so I was in the right frame of mind."

"Did it work?"

"It did until I got a look at you," he said. "Now I'm ready to turn tail and run."

"No one's allowed to run," a voice said from behind us.

"Sebastian," I said, holding out my hand to his. "I thought you were tied up at home getting ready for Ali's graduation."

"Are you kidding me? And miss this?" he said with a big grin on his face.

"You're actually excited about it?" I asked and then thought, *It figured*. Leave it to Sebastian to find some sort of fucking silver lining when the rest of us knew the reality.

"What's not to be excited about? This is huge! Come on. Levi's probably waiting on us." Sebastian shook Declan's hand and then took the lead on the walk across the parking lot.

"Freak," I mumbled under my breath as I finally convinced my legs to move and follow.

If I thought I was freaking out in the car before, it was nothing to how I felt ten minutes later. The smells. The sights. It was my own personal hell on earth at the moment. I was on the verge of getting pulled under when suddenly a hand on my back and the sound of my name brought me back.

"Cole! Thanks for coming, man. Seriously. I'm really glad you're here!"

And there was Levi. Standing there in a set of scrubs, looking like he hadn't slept in a week, and wearing the goofiest grin on his face I had ever seen.

"Congratulations," I finally said and shook his hand.

"Thanks." His grin seemed to get even bigger. Looking around the waiting room, Levi was larger than life as he took in the three of us. "I have to tell you, I thought I was a strong man, but after watching Harper go through what she just did, I realized we don't have anything on her. She was amazing!"

"Speak for yourself," I said with a laugh. "Her body is designed to do that. What's the big deal?"

His smile didn't even falter. "Trust me. I know what we all went through in our training and in the field but..." He stopped and shook his head. "I've never seen anything like it. It was just incredible. I'm humbled. Seriously. I always knew Harper was strong, but after this? I have a whole new respect for her."

"As well you should," Declan said. "You're the reason she had to go through that."

We all laughed. "Yeah, well, I'm told that someday she'll look back on this and won't remember the pain. But while it was going on, she was one tiny, pissed-off woman."

"You would be too if you were trying to get another human being out of your body," Seb joked. We all quieted down then and just sat in amicable silence for a moment. "So when can we see her?"

"Actually, Harper's sleeping right now. She's exhausted. We sent the baby down to the nursery just so Harper could catch a couple of hours of sleep. I thought we could walk down the hall and you can at least see him."

"Him?" I asked. *Crap.* I hadn't even asked what the baby was. Hadn't really wanted to know. When Sebastian had called earlier, Harper was still in labor.

We all stood, and Levi's big grin was back. "Uh-huh. A boy."

There was more backslapping and handshakes and shouts of congratulations as we walked down the hall toward the nursery. The guys were all talking, but all I could hear was a loud buzzing in my head.

It's a boy.
It's a boy.
It's a boy.

Stopping in front of the window of the nursery, Levi motioned to one of the nurses, and she smiled as she complied. A minute later, she was standing on the other side of the glass with a tiny baby swaddled in blue.

"Guys, I'd like to introduce you to my son, Gavin," Levi said quietly.

I couldn't speak. Hell, the words almost seemed to come out strangled from Levi. It wasn't about how much time had gone by. He was still a part of us. And now thanks to the birth of the baby we were all staring at, he was going to continue to be a part of all of us in a new way.

I wasn't sure if that was a good or a bad thing.

Levi shared the baby's weight and length and all the other stuff new dads boast and brag about. I was only half listening. I was studying the kid. He didn't look like much.

Tiny. Red. Wrinkly. I didn't see a family resemblance in either direction, but I suppose that would come with time.

I could only pray he didn't resemble Gavin—our Gavin—too much. That would just be weird. Plus it could be hard on Harper and her parents. What would they be feeling right now? If I was still struggling with this shit, it must be ten times harder for them. Would they see this baby as an extension of their son? Would they be able to differentiate between the two? Crap, I couldn't even imagine.

Strange as it sounds, I couldn't seem to take my eyes off the kid. He looked like he was sleeping, and he was pretty much wrapped up like a burrito and had a small knit hat on, but he was oddly hypnotic to watch. Hard to imagine how just a couple of hours ago, that baby was still inside Harper. *Yikes.* Not an image I needed to have. A full shudder wracked my body when suddenly it felt like everyone was staring at me.

"What?" I asked, looking at the three expectant faces staring at me. "What'd I do?"

"Have you been listening at all?" Levi asked.

"Uh..." Declan and Sebastian each turned away and snickered, and suddenly I was suspicious. How much could they have said? I wasn't staring at the kid that long, was I?

Levi motioned for Seb and Declan to turn around, and then they were all facing me again. "Look," Levi began, "we needed to talk to you about something, and we all agreed that this was the perfect setting because you aren't allowed to freak out here."

"Says who?" I snapped. As soon as my voice rose, it seemed like there were a dozen people shushing me from every direction.

Declan chuckled. "Seriously, you need to hear us out and keep yourself in control and remember where we are."

Now I was more than suspicious. I was pissed. I was being set up for something, and by the sound of it, I wasn't going to like it. Straightening, I took a deep breath and then ground my molars until I was sure they were going to crack. "Fine."

"Obviously, I'm not taking any cases for a while. Harper and I discussed it, and I want to be home with her and the baby for at least the first month. Seb has Ali's graduation, and then he has vacation time coming to him. And Dec…"

"Yeah, yeah, yeah." I huffed. "I get it. New case. It's mine. Whatever. Spit it out, Levi. What's the situation?"

Now it was his turn to sigh as if bracing himself, and if I wasn't mistaken, Sebastian and Declan moved closer to him—as if they were presenting a united front against me. *Shit.*

"Hollywood actress…"

"No." I interrupted. "No way. Uh-uh. Get one of the new guys. I'm not babysitting some spoiled diva, sprinkling her with glitter and carrying her tiara and shit."

"Dude, do you even think before you let the words come out?" Declan asked. "Tiara? For real?"

"What? It's a thing."

"Yeah, the only difference is she's not a Disney princess. Get serious."

"Fine. Whatever. Why am I the one who has to do this, rather than one of the new guys?"

"Because it's an important case," Levi said seriously. "Yes, she's a Hollywood actress, but she's also a childhood friend of Sebastian's."

"So why can't he do it?" I demanded. "I mean, I already know about Ali's graduation and their vacation, but seriously? Shouldn't he be the one to do it?"

"Conflict of interest," Sebastian interjected. "There's no way I could do this objectively. You know that."

Yeah, I did. But I didn't have to like it. "Whatever. So... what? She needs someone to stand by her door and make sure her adoring fans don't bother her? I'm telling you now, if she has one of those stupid, tiny, yappy dogs, I'm not carrying it!"

"Somebody's been watching too much TMZ." Declan snickered.

"Fuck you."

"Okay, let's reel it in here." Levi interrupted. "It's not just a simple case of needing a bodyguard. She already has one. The problem is... things are getting through to her that shouldn't."

"Like what? Publisher's Clearing House bogging her down? Fan mail she doesn't want to deal with personally?"

"Threats," Sebastian said firmly. "Things have been happening while she works, and things are showing up at her house that are suspect. We're definitely dealing with a stalker situation, and her staff isn't getting anywhere. She's scared, and she needs the best. That's you, Cole."

"Flattery isn't going to help here," I growled, hating every detail about the case already.

"I don't give a shit about flattering you. I care about Evangeline."

"*Evangeline?* That's her fucking name? Who does that to a kid?"

"Look, forget about her name," Levi said with some exasperation. "She's going to be in Baltimore filming a movie, and you need to be there to secure the set and see if you can find what her security team is missing. Obviously, they're not on top of it like they need to be, and that's why things have escalated to this point. Evangeline is starting to get freaked out. Her safety is our top priority."

"Yeah, but—"

"No. There's nothing for you to say here," Levi said in a tone I knew meant he was done listening. "It's a case that needs to be kept out of the press because we don't want a media circus, and I know that's right up your alley—keeping things out of the spotlight. I need to know you're committed to this, Cole. No fucking around."

"I'm not going to put up with some diva and her crazy-ass demands," I said. "I'm not making sure her dog has a raincoat or… or… or she only has blue M&M's in her candy dish or that her dressing room smells like fucking sunshine. As long as none of that shit is in my job description, we'll be fine."

Although I couldn't tell who it was, someone chuckled. "Fine. We'll be sure that all those things are clear. She arrives in town Tuesday. That gives you a couple of days to get yourself together and do a walk-through of where they'll be filming. Sebastian has the file with all the pertinent information." Once he was done, Levi turned toward the nursery and once again motioned for the nurse. "Now if you guys will excuse me, I'm going to see if my wife is awake so we can have some time together with our son. Feel free to come back up in about an hour. I'm sure she'd love to see you." And with that he was gone.

Sure, he gets to walk away and toward his perfect life.

Bastard.

"The file's out in my car," Sebastian said, coming up beside me. "Why don't we go down to the cafeteria and grab some coffee and talk a little more about the case before coming back up here."

It was on the tip of my tongue to flip him off and leave. After all, I didn't ask for this, and I certainly wasn't in the mood for it. Just like I wasn't in the mood to come back up here and make goo-goo faces at a baby. But I liked Harper. Plus Gavin was like a brother to me, so I kind of felt obligated to do it.

Do it for me.

Yeah, yeah, I said to myself. I'd do it. I'd hate every second of it, but I'd come back up here and do what was expected. I'd even try to look like I was enjoying myself by plastering a smile on my face. Maybe I'd stop in the gift shop and buy a teddy bear or flowers or some shit to really hammer the joy home.

But once I left here today, I'd consider my obligation filled. They all got to leave here—Declan, Sebastian and Levi—and go home to their happy little lives, while all I had to go home to were empty rooms and memories.

And to start my research on some pampered diva with an overinflated ego who was probably just mistaking an adoring fan for something more dramatic. Probably a publicity stunt, no matter how much she claims she wanted it kept out of the press. Well, she was in for one hell of a surprise, because once she got a look at me and heard what I had to say, she'd realize that I was not a babysitter to the rich and famous, and I didn't do coddling.

And I certainly didn't care about making a scene.

ONE

Evangeline

A small group of preteen girls squealed as I got out of the chauffeured car and tried to hurry into the back door of an old apartment building in downtown Baltimore. The building had been vacant for more than a year and had been leased for the next month to use as the primary set for my new film.

The group of squealers was a normal collection of my fans—maybe eight or ten fresh-faced girls thrusting out various objects for me to sign. My assistant, Cali, had told me on the ride over how the location of the film set had been leaked on one of my fan sites, but only the die-hard fans would manage to talk their parents or older siblings into hauling them over here before eight in the morning.

The girls didn't normally bother me, except I had a headache, and the high-pitched squeals didn't help.

I'd been the star of a popular teenaged cable show all through my teens—singing and dancing and overacting my way through the life experiences of a girl who stumbled clumsily into Broadway stardom—and it was hard to shake that image and the fans who came along with it.

It might actually be impossible, although I was trying.

I signed autographs for a minute, keeping the fake, bright smile on my face until Cali said we had to get inside, and I breathed a sigh of relief when the noise was shut outside.

I needed coffee and ibuprofen and a little quiet, but I was likely to just get the first two.

"Evangeline. There you are."

I turned to see Jimmy, my longtime manager, walking over from the donuts laid out on the craft service table. Twelve years ago, when my parents had hired him in the hopes that I would become a star, he'd had such a laid-back and paternal air that I'd immediately liked him, and nothing had changed in the intervening years.

"Everything okay?" he asked, studying my face.

I hadn't gotten much sleep last night, and it probably showed on my face. "I'm fine. A headache."

Cali jumped into action to get me some pills while Jimmy glanced around the old, no-frills building—a far cry from the Hollywood studios I was used to. Most of the interior shots for the film would be done here and in an alley just outside, and then we'd film on location throughout Baltimore for the rest of them.

"What do you think?" Jimmy asked, still watching my face. He might act laid-back, but he was the most observant man I'd ever met.

I shrugged. "I'm not looking for luxury here. I'm looking for a change."

"Well, this is definitely going to be a change for you."

I'd agreed to a role in this gritty independent film because it was totally different from everything I'd done before. After the cable show ended, I'd made a couple of albums and toured the country, doing major concerts and appearances. Then I'd starred in a movie—a big-budget musical—and then done a prime-time sitcom that had been canceled after one season. I could have done another musical or an over-the-top romantic comedy that traded on my teenage reputation, but I wanted to be stretched, to prove to the world I could do more than dress in purple and belt out a peppy song. So when I was offered the role of a good girl who gets pulled into a bleak world of drug addiction and crime when she falls for the wrong guy, written by an edgy screenplay writer who was getting increasing acclaim, I decided to go for it—since no one in the world thought I could do it.

Maybe I couldn't do it, but I was sure as hell going to try.

Cali came back with pills for my headache and a bottle of water, so I gulped them down and asked for coffee.

"So everything was all right last night?" Jimmy asked.

I knew what he was asking. "Yeah. No incidents."

"Incidents" was how we referred to the threats I'd been getting—notes, packages, a couple of phone calls. I'd been hoping they would stop when I came to Baltimore, assuming the asshole was located in LA. But the night I'd arrived, I'd been delivered a bouquet of dead roses, so whoever was doing it wasn't discouraged by the distance.

That's when I'd called Sebastian.

"That's good. It doesn't look like you got much sleep though."

"I didn't. Too on edge. But maybe I'll look more in character for this role—with the bloodshot eyes and all."

"Your eyes aren't bloodshot," Cali said from beside me. "You look beautiful."

Cali would have said that whether it was true or not, so the words weren't particularly encouraging.

I was blessed with good skin, vibrant red hair, and a slender, shapely body. I didn't really think I was particularly special in the looks department, but I was often included on lists of beautiful people or hot actresses. Today, however, was definitely *not* my most attractive day.

"It doesn't matter. You won't be shooting anything today anyway." Jimmy was moving me toward my dressing room. "You need to take care of yourself though." He glanced over at Cali. "Get her a massage or something for later today, will you?"

Cali nodded and started working on her ever-present phone.

I sighed. I wouldn't mind a massage, but it wasn't really going to fix anything.

I had some sort of stalker who kept sending me increasingly nasty threats. It made me feel sick, exposed, completely vulnerable. And if this film was a flop, I'd have to go back to singing for the teenyboppers since it would be a sign I wasn't really equipped to do anything else.

And all the massages in the world weren't going to change either of those things.

~

I was finishing my coffee in the dressing room a few minutes later when my phone chirped.

Cali usually took possession of my phone while I was working, but I grabbed it before she could snatch it away.

Sebastian's name popped up with a text that said simply, "He's on his way."

Irrationally, I felt a little better.

I'd grown up with Sebastian. Our families had been friends, and we'd gone to the same exclusive schools since kindergarten although he was two years older than me. We'd even dated some as teenagers, when I was back home in DC between filming seasons.

Nothing had ever been serious between us, but he felt like family, and I was glad I'd made the decision to contact him about my problem. When he'd gotten out of the Marines, he'd started up a security firm with some of his buddies, and I couldn't help but envy the way he'd broken away from the pressure of his family and made his own way in the world.

That was what I wanted too—to not give in to the demands of everyone around me, who wanted me to be a perky princess who made everyone a lot of money. I wanted to really be *me*. Just me. If Sebastian could do his own thing, maybe I could too.

It was just taking me longer.

"Sebastian's guy is on his way," I told Cali, who was waiting expectantly for me to report. "Maybe you can go catch him when he arrives and bring him back here."

"Sure. Malcolm doesn't like him."

"Well, Malcolm isn't going to like him no matter what since he thinks he's treading on his territory. I can explain that I just want someone else to help with the stalker situation, but Malcolm is still going to think I don't trust him."

"Do you trust him?"

I shrugged. "I think so. He's always done a fine job. I just don't know why they can't get control of this guy. Another person on the job can only help, so Malcolm is just going to have to suck up his hurt feelings."

"Should I tell him that?" There was almost a smile on Cali's face.

"Please don't. Just go wait for this guy, will you?"

Cali nodded and left the room, and I went to stretch out on the small couch against the wall. The day hadn't even started, and I was already exhausted. I wondered if anyone would notice if I just collapsed on the couch and took a nap.

My head felt a little better when I closed my eyes.

A few minutes later, there was a tap on the door, and I opened my eyes slowly, not wanting to jar the headache back.

Cali opened the door—she was used to not always waiting for a response—so I hadn't even turned my head when there were two people standing in the dressing room.

Cali was one.

And the guy was another.

When Sebastian said he had a buddy who was better at security than anyone he'd ever known, I'd expected the man to be kind of like Sebastian. Clean-cut. Articulate. Maybe even handsome.

This guy wasn't any of those things.

He was strong, with impressive shoulders and suppressed power in his stance. But he looked rough, unshaven, with a square jaw and steel-gray eyes that were strangely challenging.

He didn't look anything like Sebastian. He didn't look anything like the guys I was used to seeing.

He looked like he belonged in this dark, gritty, crime drama I was acting in now. He could have been the lead.

All this flashed through my head in the few seconds I blinked at him until I realized I was supine on the little couch in my leggings and tunic-style top, which was presently riding up too high.

Pulling myself together, I sat up and smiled at him—my normal, friendly smile with which I always greeted new people. "Hi. I'm Evangeline. Thanks for coming out."

The guy gave a grunt that might have been a word—but not an identifiable one.

Feeling annoyed that he couldn't even stretch himself enough to smile, I stood up, wincing slightly when my headache came back with full force. I reached a hand out to him, a gesture he was forced to return in order to shake my hand.

His grip was strong, warm—almost uncomfortably firm. It felt just as challenging as his gaze did.

"So Sebastian gave you the background and everything?" I asked, deciding that getting down to business made the most sense since this guy clearly didn't want to be friendly.

"Yes. I've done my homework."

I waited to hear about what homework he'd done, but he didn't offer any details. His eyes raked over me, leaving me feeling almost naked.

What was with this guy's attitude anyway?

"Okay. Any thoughts then?"

"Not yet, but I just got here." His eyes narrowed, and they shifted from me to the rest of the dressing room—which was small and simple with none of the luxury I was used to. His gaze rested on the large bouquet of roses and orchids, which Jimmy had ordered for me to brighten up the sparse room.

"Okay," I said again, feeling half-awkward and half-annoyed. Now, I was the first to admit that my life had been privileged in a lot of ways, and people probably went out of their way to please me—just based on my fame and my money. But I couldn't believe this guy's rudeness would be acceptable, no matter who he was talking to. "Just so you know, my current security isn't too happy about the fact that I brought you in."

"I could tell. But you shouldn't get in a fuss about that since your staff could be part of the problem."

"What?" My response was torn between annoyance at his patronizing tone in saying I might "make a fuss" and concern about the idea that my staff was a problem. "What are you talking about?"

"There might be a reason why the threats keep getting through to you, even though you should have more than enough protection. You need to look at your staff."

I stiffened my shoulders, really bothered by this idea. Obviously, it had occurred to me as a possibility, but I only had a small number of people who worked for me, and they'd all been with me for years. I couldn't believe any of them would be responsible for something so nasty—something obviously intended to hurt me.

It made me even more scared. Even more vulnerable.

"This is why you brought me in," the guy said tersely. "Getting pissy about it isn't going to help."

I blinked, trying to figure out what he was talking about. Maybe it was the headache, or maybe it was because people normally went out of their way to be nice to me, but it took me several seconds to realize he thought I was being pissy.

He thought *I* was being pissy.

I sucked in a sharp breath. "There's no reason to talk that way to me. And I wasn't inclined to be pissy until you came in here with an attitude."

"There's no attitude." He met my eyes and seemed to tower over me, although I was tall and he was only a few inches taller. "I'm here to do a job. I don't waste my time with sugarcoating things. I'll keep you safe, and I'll find out who's doing this to you, but I don't cater to divas or prima donnas."

I was so shocked and outraged that I almost sputtered. I felt my cheeks blaze hot, and my fingers tightened at my sides. I actually wanted to slug this guy. I couldn't remember the last time I fought that particular instinct.

Before I could get any word spoken—much less the frigid setdown his obnoxiousness deserved—Cali reappeared in the doorway.

"They want you out front for the read-through," she said, looking curiously between the two of us as if she'd sensed something was off.

I cleared my throat. "I'll talk to you later," I said to the guy, hoping I sounded appropriately dismissive. "What's your name anyway?"

He'd moved to leave immediately, but he paused at my last question. Turning his head to give me a cool look, he said, "Cole."

Cole. The name fit him somehow.

Deciding the thing that would annoy him the most was to not react to his rudeness, I had a sudden inspiration.

"If you'll excuse me, Cole," I said with my sweetest of smiles, "we can talk later."

He blinked, looking briefly surprised, but then he narrowed his eyes as he shot me one last look and left the room.

I blew out a sigh as I watched his tight butt and strong back leave the room.

As soon as I got a break, I was going to call Sebastian. There was no way I was going to put up with this asshole for more than a day.

~

"Just give him some time," Sebastian said, sounding like he was smiling on the other end of the phone. "It takes a while to warm up to him, but Cole is a good guy."

"I don't care what kind of goodness is buried beneath the surface. I don't have time or patience to try to find it. I need help now, and this guy is rude and hostile and inappropriate, and I don't want him hanging around me." I was alone in my dressing room now after a first read-through, but I glared at the closed door, where Cole had been standing earlier that morning.

"He's all we can send you. The rest of us are booked up right now."

"Why can't you come out? I'd much rather have you here."

"I know, but it's just not going to work right now. Cole is just as good as I am. Better, probably. If anyone can take care of this business for you, it's him."

"Well, can't you tell him to try to be nice? I'm under enough stress without putting up with his attitude."

"I'll talk to him."

"It's not like we have to be friends, but I don't think it's too much to expect some basic courtesy."

Sebastian chuckled. "It might be too much to expect out of Cole, but I'll talk to him."

"I mean, normal people don't pick a fight on first meeting someone. It's like he has something against me, before he's even really met me."

"It's not personal. It's just his way."

"Well, he needs to change his way, because I'm not going to put up with it." I wasn't sure why I was getting so riled up about the guy. A two-minute conversation shouldn't have bugged me so much. I breathed out, telling myself to calm down and not get so bothered by something so unimportant.

"He really got on your bad side quick. You're usually pretty easygoing."

"I know! But I'm telling you he was horrible. I'll pay you double if you come out and send him away."

Sebastian laughed out loud. "I'm sorry, Evangeline. But it has to be Cole. What's he doing now anyway?"

"I don't know. He's probably interrogating my staff some more. My assistant said he gave her the third degree for almost an hour. I mean, Cali has been with me since I was thirteen. Does he think she's suddenly turned into some sort of crazed stalker?"

"He's probably just trying to get background information. Be patient. I promise Cole will be able to help."

"He better. Okay, I've got to get going."

"I'll talk to Cole and tell him to try to rein in his worst instincts."

"There's going to be an awful lot to rein in," I muttered, before I said goodbye and hung up.

This whole situation sucked. It was bad enough to know someone was threatening me.

It was even worse to have to put up with a guy like Cole in order to keep myself safe.

I honestly wasn't sure which was worse.

TWO
Cole

"If you're calling to check up on me and lecture me on catering to your little princess friend, I'm not interested." As soon as I'd seen Sebastian's name on my phone, I knew he was calling to bitch at me. Well, maybe not bitch but certainly to lecture. No doubt the diva had called and cried because I didn't bow down and fall all over myself in her presence.

Worst. Job. Ever.

"Man, don't you ever get tired of being such a pain in the ass?" Sebastian asked wearily. "I mean, honestly, it's exhausting for the rest of us to have to deal with you. Why can't you just, you know, be normal?"

"I hate to break it to you, but this is normal for me. If she's already running to you and crying, that's her problem. I'm not here to be her friend or part of her fan club. I've got a job to do."

"I get it, Cole, but can't you do the job without being so freaking difficult?"

"How was I being difficult? She finally arrives here, and after playing the giggly schoolgirl with her fan club, she allows me to hold court with her. I walk into her dressing room and she's napping. Fucking napping! It was only like… nine in the morning! Who does that?"

Sebastian sighed. "Who cares? You didn't have to be rude to her."

I was just about ready to punch something. "I wasn't rude. I was me. That's it. I walked in, I took in the surroundings, and looked for anything that was maybe a little... off. She wanted to play at being the happy hostess, and I wasn't in the mood. Like I said, I've got a job to do, and she needs to respect that and stop being so damn sensitive."

"Okay, fine. Whatever. What are your thoughts so far?"

"Her security team is a joke. Honestly. They all like her, and as long as they're just dealing with screaming teenage girls and only have to stand there like a wall, they're fine. None of them are trained for anything beyond that. I've seen mall security with higher training."

"Fabulous. Now what?"

"I'm going to work with the guys a bit to teach them what they need to be looking for, and I've suggested they all work on their... shall we say... physical fitness."

"What the hell does that mean?"

"It means they're big but not in a way that's going to help anyone if we have to actually move and run."

Silence.

"They're fat, Sebastian. They've been riding the diva's coattails and spending too much time around the catering truck, eating donuts. They're in no shape to do much good if someone physically came around and threatened her."

Sebastian snickered.

"What? What's so funny?"

"You're just like Declan was."

"What do you mean?"

"When he was on the case where he met Kristin and he was guarding the child pageant star. He refused to say her name, and you're doing the same exact thing."

I swiped a hand across my face and sighed loudly. "It's a ridiculous name."

"You're going to have to say it eventually. You cannot keep on with referring to Evangeline as 'her' or 'the princess' or 'the diva'."

"How about pain in the ass? Can I use that one?"

"Not funny, Cole. I'm serious. Evangeline is a close friend—practically family—and I need to know you're committed to taking care of her."

"I'm here, aren't I?"

"Yeah, but under protest. I need you to let go of why you don't want to be there and put your energy into finding out who's threatening her."

The thing is, I knew he was right. I knew I needed to quit feeling so defensive and do what I was being paid to do, but everything about this case just bugged me. This person… this… *Evangeline*… grew up with every creature comfort and privilege a kid could want. She was rich and famous by the time she was twelve. She had no idea what it was like to struggle for anything.

Even now with this stalker situation, she was still very protected, and there was still the possibility of this being more a nuisance than a genuine danger. And she didn't even have to deal with it herself—she was paying other people to take care of it for her.

"Cole?"

"Yeah, what? I'm here."

"You got quiet," Sebastian said, the weariness back in his voice. "Look, I really want to be able to trust you on this. We've got Ali's graduation this weekend, and I'm trying to keep her calm and focused. This trip we're going on is a surprise, and that's where I need my attention to be, so please, man. Do this for me. Tone down the attitude and just... find out who's scaring Evangeline."

Every time Sebastian said her name, I wanted to snort with disgust. Such a stupid name. I pushed the thought aside and focused on Seb. He was a good guy, and he'd had my back more times than I probably deserved. "Okay. Fine. I'll lighten up a bit. But know this, I'm taking this job seriously, and that means I need to focus and not be bothered stroking this chick's ego. Tell her to do her job, and I'll do mine, and hopefully we won't need to be in each other's faces hardly at all."

"I suppose that's all I can ask for."

"Yeah, it is."

"Keep me posted. I'm going to be around until Saturday night. Our flight leaves at eight, and then I'd like to be able to put the phone away for a couple of days, if you know what I mean."

"Uh, sure. Luckily, I was able to crack that code," I said sarcastically. "Don't worry about things here. Go and be the doting fiancé, and I've got things covered on my end. If anything comes up, I'll reach out to Levi or Declan."

"But if it's really serious..."

"Seb, I get it. She's your friend, and you're concerned. I'm on it. Go and enjoy yourself, and tell Ali congratulations."

"Thanks. I appreciate it. And Cole?"

"Yeah?"

"I owe you."

I chuckled as I hung up and mumbled, "You have no idea."

~

The problem I was seeing with the entire situation so far was that there were way too many people around. This set claimed to be "closed," but it was in the middle of freaking downtown Baltimore. The first days just on the primary set were bad enough—especially the alley scenes—but then they would start filming elsewhere in Baltimore, where it would get a hundred times worse. There was no way to keep things completely under control in the middle of this circus.

Last count there were about a hundred people on the film crew milling around, and that didn't include the actors and their entourages, the extras, and the food people, and whoever else got a day pass to be here. It was a nightmare.

I walked the perimeter of the set. They weren't even filming today. They were just getting ready and setting up for tomorrow. The cast was off in a locked room reading lines. I hadn't seen… Evangeline… since this morning. Sebastian's words came back to haunt me, and I knew he was right. I had to address her by name and be a professional, but that name just didn't roll off the tongue, you know?

The production company had their own security people, and I managed to get some time with them to discuss what could be done to secure the area a little more. Their head guy was a little annoyed with my presence, but I really didn't care. By the time I'd walked away from him, he knew better than to second-guess me.

He would have extra men on site tomorrow when the cameras started to roll.

I stalked back over to the main building, and I found Malcolm—Evangeline's head security guy—standing outside the door of the room where the cast was reading. I could tell he puffed out his chest a little more. As if that was going to intimidate me. *Asshole.*

"Are they coming out anytime soon?" I asked him.

He shrugged.

"Have they come out at all since I've been gone?"

A head shake.

I was in no mood for this. In less time than it took to blink, I was on this guy with my arm at his throat and his body slammed against the wall. "You can give me the silent treatment on your own time. While we're here on the set, you'll talk to me when I speak to you. If you were doing your job, I wouldn't need to be here. But you're not. So why don't you give your overinflated ego a break and tell me what I need to know so we can both wrap this shit up."

The guy's eyes were defiant, but he was turning red from the pressure I had on his throat. I pressed a little harder just because I could. "We're both trying to keep her safe, so if you give a damn about her, you'll cooperate."

Then I let him go and stepped back and tried not to smirk when he gasped for air and almost sagged to the ground.

"Fine," he wheezed. "They should be coming out for lunch in a few minutes."

"Does she eat with the cast and crew or go to her dressing room?"

"Dressing room. Cali brings her the food."

"Figures," I muttered and raked a hand through my hair.

As if reading my mind, Malcolm straightened and said, "It's not like that. Evangeline used to sit out and eat with everyone and joke around. Since things started happening, it was agreed upon that she should eat in her dressing room. She hates it, but one of us usually stays with her."

"Okay, here's what I need from you—when they come out for lunch, send Cali to get her food, and you escort her to the dressing room. I'm going to spend the lunch break with her and get some background information. While I'm in there, I want you and your guys casually observing anyone who's lingering around here."

"Lingering?"

"Yeah, you know, hanging around and watching for her."

"How long of a list do you want? I mean, there's a small entourage that is always around."

"Consisting of...?"

"Besides the rest of the cast? You've got producers, directors, their assistants, makeup people... Seriously man, there's a lot."

"Okay. That's a start. But I want you to take note of who stays around longer than they need to."

Malcolm nodded and seemed to have caught his breath finally. "What if we do? Should we scare them off?"

I shook my head. "Take notes. I don't want anyone to know they're being observed. Yet. For now, I want to get a feel for what we're dealing with. See who's around and see if it's a onetime thing. We'll play it like this for a few days, and see what we can find. After a day or two, you'll eat with her, and I'll stay out and observe. Okay?"

He nodded again. "Look, Cole... you have to understand. I've been with Evangeline for years. She's like a sister to me. It pisses me off that I can't get a handle on this situation."

"I understand your frustration. I really do. But you have to know that my being here is because she needs more help. I can't have you off pouting because I'm here. We need to work together on this."

I would have said more, but the door to the reading room opened and people started milling out. Evangeline spotted Malcolm first and smiled at him—immediately going to his side. For some reason, it bothered me. She smiled at him—a relaxed smile—and wrapped her arm around his as she waved goodbye to the other actors and promised to see them in an hour.

Then she spotted me, and all that peace and relaxation immediately disappeared. She frowned and, if I wasn't mistaken, glared. Huh. Who knew she had it in her? She almost looked intimidating.

Or maybe she was just a really good actress.

Somehow I doubted it.

Either way, I stepped back and observed. Sure enough, Cali went rushing by toward the food table while Malcolm led the princess away. I leaned against the wall and did my best to blend in and observe. So far no one was lingering or looking out of place. Everyone was on the move to one place or another.

Out of the corner of my eye, I saw Malcolm open the dressing room door and usher Evangeline inside and shut the door. I'd decided to wait until I saw Cali heading back this way before going to the dressing room. Why? One, it gave me extra time out here to get a good look at how people behave, and two, I didn't want to spend any more time in that room than I absolutely had to.

I was bored already. There was nothing going on that was raising any red flags. People were busy doing their thing, and nothing seemed out of place. Obviously, someone was sending this stuff to Evangeline, but on the surface, there weren't any obvious suspects. Not that it was unusual. It just meant that this case wasn't going to be as cut and dry or as quick as I'd like it to be.

"Hey, Cole," Cali said as she approached, carrying two plates, a young mousy girl on her heels. "This is Janelle. She's one of the director's assistants. There are two. Her and Matt. You'll be seeing them around a lot, delivering scripts and scheduling changes directly to Evangeline." The girl said a quick hello before looking down at the ground. "I know we didn't talk about it, but I had a feeling you'd probably want to spend a little more time talking with Evangeline during the lunch break. I brought you a plate too."

Color me surprised. No one really took the time to think about me. I normally fended for myself. I could feel myself scowling at her and forced myself to relax. "Thanks," I murmured and motioned for her and the quiet chick to lead the way to the dressing room.

I opened the door when we got there—without knocking—and let Cali enter first. In less than a minute, our plates were set out, and both Cali and Malcolm left without hardly uttering a word. Janelle stayed for a minute and went over the revised schedule for the afternoon before scurrying from the room. Once the door closed, I turned and faced Evangeline and instantly noticed that she didn't look pleased.

"So, Emmeline, how'd the reading go?" I asked casually, walking across the room to the table where our lunch was waiting.

"It's Evangeline," she corrected but stayed standing on the opposite side of the room.

"Whatever," I said as I took my seat and eyed the giant sandwich and potato salad Cali had plated up for me. The food definitely looked good, and if I was any kind of gentleman, I'd wait for her to sit down.

But I wasn't.

She stood there and stewed for a solid minute, and I was three bites into my lunch before she finally walked over and took her seat. She was looking pretty annoyed and... prissy. I couldn't help but snort and chuckle.

"What's so funny?" she demanded.

"You. Why don't you take the stick out of your ass for a few minutes? It might make sitting easier."

"What?" Then she huffed. "You're a real jackass, you know that, right?"

"And there's no fish stinking up the room, so lose the face too."

"Excuse me?" she snapped, clearly offended.

Putting my sandwich down, I leaned in a little closer. "Look, Maybelline, you asked for protection from my company, and you've got it. By sitting here and treating me like I'm something beneath you, all you're doing is making yourself look foolish. You don't think I'm worthy of being in your presence? That's fine with me. I'm not thrilled with being in yours either. But while I am, you damn well better lose the attitude."

I could see her lush little mouth trying to form words. I didn't care. I went back to my sandwich. It was actually quite good. Ham, Swiss, a little of the spicy brown mustard that I happened to enjoy and...

"Screw you."

Now *that* got my attention. How adorable. The actress was trying to offend me. Once again, my sandwich got put down as I leaned back, crossed my arms, and studied her. "Screw you? That's all you got?"

"Unlike you, I don't need to be vulgar."

"Sweetheart, I haven't even *begun* to be vulgar around you. When it happens, you'll know."

"Every time you open your mouth, you're vulgar." She picked up her fork and stabbed it into her salad, believing she'd gotten the last word.

She thought wrong.

"I've actually been on my best behavior all day," I said sweetly. "If you don't believe me, listen to this." I paused for dramatic effect. "I've looked all around this fucking dump of a movie set. Your security team is a bunch of overweight, overpaid pussies. Not one of them is man enough to take down even one of your teenybopper fans lining the fence outside. By the time Malcolm or one of his guys got to you if the stalker got through, they'd find you either getting slashed or fucked." I stopped and raised a brow at her. "Vulgar enough for you?"

She paled. I kind of felt guilty—since a scenario like that wasn't anything to joke about—but I needed her to see the difference.

"Like I said, I wasn't vulgar earlier. I'm here to do a job, and worrying about proper etiquette and being politically correct aren't going to help."

Once again she tried to find a comeback and failed.

Good.

"Are you going to be in the room with the cast for the rest of the day?"

She nodded.

"Okay. For today, Malcolm will be outside the door while I finish getting a feel for what's going to be going on around the set. When you're done with the reading, I'll have Malcolm bring you back here so we can discuss how tomorrow is going to go. I want you to be aware of anyone who's hanging around unnecessarily. You need to be prepared for the fact that we're going to be changing things on a daily basis. If whoever is watching you doesn't know your routine, he can't get to you."

She nodded again, but her eyes were as cold as ice as she looked at me.

"So you understand what I'm doing, right?" I asked, anxious to finish my lunch.

"Yes," she said quietly.

We ate the remainder of our meal in silence.

~

Reading must have been exhausting because when I met up with Evangeline later in the day to talk to her, Cali, Malcolm and his team, she looked ready to drop.

Not my problem.

"Okay, you're due on the set tomorrow morning early, I'm told," I said, looking directly at Evangeline. When she nodded, I added, "I want you here thirty minutes before that."

"Thirty?" she objected. "That's..."

"Five o'clock. In the morning. I'm aware."

"But it's ridiculous! Why would I want to be here that early in the morning?"

All eyes were on me, I could feel it, but my eyes never left Evangeline's. "Because everyone has a copy of the schedule for tomorrow. That means if your stalker is part of the cast, crew, or whatever, or even if he gets a glimpse of the schedule, he'll be expecting you at five-thirty. We're going to start throwing things off."

"You can't mess with the production schedule," Cali said, sounding concerned. "It could lead to more trouble or Evangeline losing her role."

I still didn't lose eye contact. "No one's going to lose their job. All the schedule changes are going to happen so they don't have a conflict with production, and if I find it necessary to, I'll talk to the producer or the director or whoever else I need to." I don't think Evangeline has even blinked since I started talking. "Do you trust me?"

"Not a chance."

I sighed, realizing it would have been smarter to play a little nice so she would be easier to work with. But I never made smart decisions. "Do you trust me to do my job?"

"I don't know," she said.

"That's fine. You don't really know me but, believe me, you're going to learn to. And fast."

"Arrogant much?" she mumbled.

"Enough with the name calling," I said, filled with annoyance, the passing thought about playing nice completely disappearing. "I realize you're immature and all, but really, it's enough."

"*I'm* immature?" she said, her voice raising as she stood. "You're the one who keeps lashing out for no reason. What gives you the right to call me names and yet act like I'm not allowed to do the same?"

"Rubber and glue." I picked up my copy of the production schedule for the next day. "Malcolm, your guys are going to be on fan club detail in the morning. This is where I'm going to need your guys to be more observant—are we dealing with a bunch of overzealous girls or is there someone in the bunch who doesn't seem to fit? Take video or pictures or whatever you can in case we need to identify someone later on."

Malcolm nodded. "I'm on it."

"Wait," Evangeline interrupted. "Malcolm stays with me in the morning. Both he and Cali are nearby."

"Well, now you'll have me," I said and gave her a fake, tight smile.

"No," she said, her shoulders stiffening in defiance. "You go and watch the crowd. I want Malcolm with me."

"Newsflash, princess. You're not calling the shots. I am. And I say I'm going to be with you. Get used to it."

"Since I'm the one who hired you, I'm the one who gets to make the final decisions. I'll call Sebastian and get it worked out."

That was it. I reached out and grabbed her arm before she turned away. Malcolm and his guys were instantly on their feet ready to defend her. One look from me and they all relaxed. "Listen, you are *not* going to call Sebastian every time you don't get your way. This is why I called you immature. Only a child feels the need to tattle when they don't get what they want. Like it or not, I'm the guy here to protect you. Quit fighting every damn thing I do and say. I'm not asking to be your friend or confidante, but dammit, you're going to listen to me and do what I tell you. Are we clear?"

She stared at me for so long with eyes filled with such fire and hatred that I felt like she was burning my skin off. Abruptly she yanked her arm free. "If you call me a child again, when you've done nothing but act childish yourself, I promise you won't like the consequences. You have no idea how much I despise you."

Part of me was kind of impressed—since most people didn't put up much of a fight when I was trying to intimidate them—but the other part of me was just annoyed.

"Oh yeah?" I said through clenched teeth. "I don't fucking care. I guess I'll have to cancel my fan club membership and rip up my glittery card."

She was so furious she was shaking with it, but there was also a glint of tears in her eyes.

Shit.

In a flash, she pulled herself together and looked over at Malcolm. "Let's go," she said and walked away to pick up her jacket and purse. And then, as regally as any member of the royal family, she stood by the door and waited for her entourage to take their places before leaving the room.

She almost pulled it off except for her last-minute twist around to flip me off.

And damn if she didn't look sexy as hell doing it.

THREE
Evangeline

I was never going to forgive Sebastian for this.

I suppose I might have had a privileged, overindulged life, but I tried every day to be nice and not take advantage of the people around me. I sometimes spent too much money, and I'd had a few wild times in the past, but I was never one of the tabloid-princess celebrities who are always pouring money away or belittling the people around them. I don't think I'd done anything to deserve the way Cole was treating me, and at present there wasn't anything I could do to change it—except fire Sebastian and his whole company, which I was on the edge of doing all week.

I liked Sebastian, and I trusted him, and I was in a bad situation with the stalker. After I cooled down that first day, I'd determined to give it a week and then decide if I was going to get rid of the asshole.

Fortunately, Cole seemed to be not quite so offensive after the first day. He was cold and gruff and irrationally grumpy, but I figured that was his normal attitude. If he'd continued to act as horribly as he had the first day, I never would have made it through the week with him.

I was scared of the stalker, but there were other security firms out there—with men who would act like professionals—and it was only my faith in Sebastian that was keeping me from switching to one of them.

Sebastian said Cole was a good guy. So far, I hadn't seen any evidence of that.

The week was spent reading and blocking for the most part, although they filmed a few exterior scenes I wasn't a part of near the end of the week. Filming my scenes wouldn't begin until next week, and on Saturday I was looking forward to some time at home—mostly for some free time from the obnoxiousness of Cole Langham.

It wasn't really my home, of course. It was a rented, furnished apartment on the top floor of a downtown high-rise. It was going to be my home for the next month or so though, and what mattered was Cole wouldn't be anywhere around.

So it was a very unpleasant surprise when I came out from my bedroom at about nine o'clock on Saturday morning to find Cole sitting on a stool at the kitchen bar.

I was wearing a camisole and soft pajama shorts. I was barefoot, and my hair was a mess.

"What the hell are you doing here?" I demanded after a moment of shocked paralysis.

"My job." He arched one dark, annoying eyebrow at me.

"Who let you into my place?"

"Malcolm."

"Why are you here?" I did my best to moderate my tone out of general civility, but I wanted to scream and push him out of here. How dare he think he could invade my privacy for no good reason?

"There was a call last night."

"What?" I'd been about to put a mug under the high-class, one-cup brewer, but I paused and stared at him instead. "What call?"

"You had a call. It was concerning."

I felt a familiar drop to my stomach and a chill of fear. "What did it say?"

"It doesn't matter."

"It damn well does matter. Tell me what the call said."

"It was nasty, and there was mention of something else happening today, so that's why I'm here. It's sure as hell not because I wanted to get cozy with you or anything."

He didn't have to sound so offensive all the time. He made it sound like I'd actually thought he was interested in me, but there was no way in the world I could be that stupid.

He clearly disliked me as much as I disliked him.

I wasn't used to people disliking me. Sure, maybe some of them faked it since I had money and a certain degree of power—although not nearly as much power as people thought. But I don't think most people held me in aversion the way Cole seemed to do from the first moment he had met me.

Actually, he seemed to hate me *before* he'd even met me, and I had no idea why.

He wouldn't even say my name, which was petty and immature as far as I was concerned. It wasn't my real name—my real name was Eve, but my mother had decided it wasn't distinct enough to work for an up-and-coming actress, so I'd adopted the stage name that everyone used when talking to me now. But Cole wouldn't even use that.

I rolled my eyes as I waited for the coffee to brew, telling myself that on Monday I could make the decision about whether to go in a different direction with security. I could handle Cole for the weekend, and I could get rid of him Monday if I wanted.

Then something occurred to me. I whirled around. "Are you intercepting my phone calls?" I demanded.

He arched his eyebrow at me again. "I said I'm doing my job."

"But what right do you have to intercept my calls without even clearing it with me first?"

"My job is to protect you and to find out who this stalker is." His voice was rough and edgy in a familiar way. He always sounded that way when he was angry with me. "I do anything I need to do to make sure that happens. No one forced you to hire us, so don't give me that poor-little-rich-girl-victim routine."

I turned back around, mostly so I didn't slap that arrogant look off his face, and I breathed deeply to control my anger.

Only until Monday. I just had to put up with him until Monday.

When I'd felt mostly under control, I turned back around, sipping my coffee. "So you're just going to hang around here all day?"

"I'm going to stay close to you. What are you plans?"

"I was just going to take it easy. I've got some work I can do here, and then I might visit a day spa this afternoon."

I should have expected the faint sneer that showed up on his face at the words. Naturally, he would think I was some sort of diva for visiting a day spa, even though my appearance was vitally important for my work, and without semiregular massages, tension would make my neck unbearably painful.

No use trying to explain any of that to Cole though.

Without another word, I took my coffee out onto the large terrace. It was beautifully furnished with outdoor seating and a table and some potted trees. There probably would have been more plants, but February wasn't an ideal time of the year for making things grow in Baltimore.

I might have hoped for something different, but I wasn't surprised when Cole followed me out onto the terrace.

"It's freezing out here," he muttered. "Get back inside."

It was chilly—probably in the forties—and I was just wearing the little pajamas I'd slept in. I would have gone back inside immediately, but some sort of contrariness sprung up inside me at his bossiness. "I'll go back inside in a minute."

"What the hell, princess?" He reached out to take my arm. "You'll freeze your tight little ass off. Get inside."

I jerked my arm out of his grip. "I'll go inside when I want. I might have to suffer having you around all the time, but you don't get to control my every step. If you're too much of a wuss to stay outside when it's nippy, you can go inside and curl up under a blanket."

He made a throaty sound but didn't articulate any words. He just stood right next to me, glaring at me.

I did my best to ignore him as I walked close to the railing, still drinking my coffee. What the hell had I been thinking coming out here without any shoes? And now I was stuck for at least a few minutes, or I'd have to admit that Cole was right.

"It's just Baltimore," Cole said, still sounding bad-tempered. "Not much of anything to stand and gawk at."

"I've never been to Baltimore before," I told him. "I grew up around DC, but I never had any reason to come out this way."

"Not much reason to come here at all."

I heard something different in his tone and glanced over to check his face. "You've been here before?"

"I grew up here."

"Oh." This was new information and vaguely interesting. I tried to keep my teeth from chattering from the cold as I asked, "What part of the city?"

"Not a good part. Definitely on the wrong side of the tracks. Pretty much exactly the opposite from where you were raised."

I could kind of see that. He had a lot of really hard edges, as if he'd had to push through a lot of crap to get where he was. Maybe that was why he hated me so much—because he thought my upbringing had all been velvet and roses, compared to his.

It helped me understand him better. Not like him any better though.

"Do you resent everyone who didn't grow up the way you did?"

He turned his head toward me. "What?"

"You seem to resent me, and it seems to be because you think I had an easier time in life than you did."

"I bet you everything in your fat wallet that you did."

I brushed off the snide comment. "Whether it's true or not, you resent me for it. That's a hard way to go through life, only respecting people you think have suffered as much as you have. Do you resent Sebastian too?"

Something flickered on his face, and I could see that he had resented Sebastian—at least at one point even if he didn't still now. "Sebastian is a friend."

"So that means you've realized there's more to him than the easy life you think he's had. Is it possible that might be true of me?"

Cole met my eyes, and for a moment he seemed to really see me. See *me*—in a way he hadn't in the entire past week. Before he could say anything, though, the buzzer from the doorman sounded.

Both of us jumped, and I ran back into the living area of the apartment, relieved to be back inside.

"Are you expecting anyone?" Cole asked as he reached to pick up the phone to talk to the doorman.

I shook my head and waited.

"I'll be right down," Cole said after a minute and hung up. He looked at me. "Jimmy sent you something from the bakery. Is that normal?"

Nodding, I said, "He normally sends me something once a week."

With a curt nod, Cole went down to get it, and he came up with a box of gourmet muffins.

I smiled at the sight. "Jimmy has sent these to me before. He does it to be nice. I'm sure it's fine." I reached out to take the box from Cole.

Cole was still frowning, but after inspecting the box from all angles, he handed it to me.

I brought it over to the counter, realizing I was a little hungry since all I'd had so far today was half a cup of coffee.

When I lifted the top, there were the familiar rows of muffins in a variety of flavors. I grabbed one and started to take a bite.

Then I noticed something. In one of the slots for the muffins, there wasn't a muffin.

There was a dead mouse.

I squealed in shock and disgust, dropped the lid, and took several steps away from the box, shuddering in disgust and spitting out the bite I'd just taken.

Cole sprang into action immediately, jumping over to examine the box and then coming over to me.

I was still spitting and half sobbing, trying to get the sight of that mouse out of my head. For some reason it was more horrifying than it should have been. I definitely didn't like mice, but when it was placed like that, amid food objects that were supposed to be a gift, it took on a kind of nightmare, surreal quality.

"Evangeline," Cole was saying, sounding urgent, strong, strangely reassuring. "Evangeline, are you all right? It's okay. It's okay."

But it wasn't okay. I ran over to the sink to fill a glass of water and swish it in my mouth, spitting it out again into the sink. There was no reason to think anything was wrong with the muffin I'd taken a bite from, but it had been in the box with the dead mouse, and I didn't want any crumb of it remaining.

"It's just to scare you," Cole said, evidently assuring himself I hadn't been poisoned and going back over to the box. He put the lid on it and moved it out of the kitchen, over to a table near the door. "It's just supposed to scare you."

"It did scare me," I said, rubbing my mouth with the back of my hand. "It was horrible."

"I know. It was ugly. I'm sorry I didn't check the box before I let you open it."

I shook my head since it was obviously not his fault. "Jimmy sends me those muffins. He's done it a lot. The note sounded like him."

Cole nodded, looking sober. "It's someone who's familiar with your and those around you."

That was even more terrifying. I gave a little whimper, shivering from the aftermath of the horror on top of the chill from being outside in my pajamas. I hugged myself, barely able to stand still.

I must have looked particularly pitiful because Cole's expression broke with what looked like empathy. "Damn it," he said, reaching out and pulling me against him, wrapping me in one of his arms. "It's over now."

It didn't feel like it was over. It felt like there was a stranger in my home, constantly threatening me, making me helpless, vulnerable.

I just wanted it to stop.

I felt better with his arm around me, and I huddled against him. He felt warm and strong, and I needed it.

After a minute, though, I started to pull myself together. I was a little embarrassed at my breakdown, particularly since it probably just confirmed Cole's first impression of me being weak and spoiled. I pulled away enough to look up at him. "Sorry," I mumbled. "I'm okay."

"You don't look okay." His eyes weren't as cold and hard as normal. They looked protective. And defiant, but not toward me.

If there was anyone I wanted going after the bastard doing this to me, it was this man. It was Cole. The bastard wouldn't have a chance against that strength and defiance.

"I'm okay," I repeated, pulling farther away from him. "Sorry about the dramatics. It was just a mouse."

"It was ugly," he said again. "Anyone would be upset by it. Fuck, I'm upset about it."

Ridiculously, that made me feel better, even though I was sure he was lying. "Thank you." I gave him a small smile and hugged myself again when another chill ran over me as my eyes glanced past the table near the door where the box was.

Cole put an arm around me again, and I let myself take comfort in it—for just a few seconds.

"I used to love getting packages in the mail," I murmured, following the line of my thoughts. "My granddad used to send me these caramels from a little candy shop in his town. He'd send them every week to me when I started doing the television show—just to let me know he was thinking about me. The only place you could get those caramels was Hillsville, Indiana, and every time they came in the mail to me, I'd know he was thinking of me. They just meant love."

I realized what I was saying—to a guy who'd been nothing but a jerk to me—so I pulled away, a little embarrassed.

"Sounds like a good grandpa," he said, not sounding like he thought I was stupid.

I nodded. "I haven't had them since he died, but getting stuff in the mail always felt really special to me because of it. But now I'm afraid it's all going to be tainted because of this."

"This won't last long. We'll get him."

When I looked up at him, his expression was different. It was still protective, but it was warm in a very different way.

I responded to the expression immediately. My heart accelerated, and my pulse started to throb in my wrists and my throat. There was something very masculine, powerful, almost fierce about him. He wasn't handsome like the men I was used to dating, but his presence so close to me suddenly prompted an instinct more primitive than anything I'd ever experienced.

As if my body was attuned to his—by nature, all the way down to the core.

We stared at each other, both of us breathing heavily, and for a moment I was sure he would kiss me.

And I wanted him to. Ridiculously, irrationally, I wanted him to.

I wanted him to claim me in some primal way.

Fortunately, my brain finally caught up, and I suddenly saw us as if from a distance. Me in my pajamas, him in his jeans and bad attitude, trapped in some sort of holding pattern of resentment and attraction for a moment that just wouldn't end.

Then I remembered everything he had said to me that week, all the offensive ways he had treated me.

There was no way in hell I could kiss that kind of man.

There was no way in hell I would want to.

I turned away, reaching for my lukewarm coffee and taking a swig, mostly for something to do.

He made a sound in his throat and took a step back too. "I'll have the box checked out," he said at last, sounding not nearly as focused as normal. "And I'll look into the courier service. This guy won't be able to hide his tracks as well as he thinks."

I nodded. "Good."

He looked around as if he wasn't sure what to do. "I'll go take care of it. You stay here today."

I didn't want to go out. I didn't want to go anywhere. But I also didn't want him to order me around as if I had no say about my own life. "I might go to the day spa later."

"No. You need to stay here today."

I stiffened in anger, more at his harsh tone than at the instructions. "I'll go somewhere if I want to. Malcolm can take me."

"No, he can't."

I snapped, completely losing my patience. After the week of aggravation and the fright I'd just had, I had no mental barriers left. Not to mention the weird reaction I'd just had to him, which I absolutely could not let myself entertain. "You can't stop me from doing normal things. It's not dangerous. I haven't made an appointment, so no one can know I'm going there. Maybe someone like you could be satisfied buried in a hole somewhere, but most of us want to behave like civilized human beings."

I regretted the words as soon as I'd said them since they came out sounding like I was slamming him for a class reason—as if he were lower-class and thus uncivilized—when

I'd intended it to be about his endlessly rude behavior. But there was nothing I could do about it now.

At least I'd said something to show how I felt about him.

He grew very still for just a minute, and then his eyes turned ice cold. "Understood," he said. "But you're still not going with Malcolm. If you're going out today, I'll get an extra guy to go too."

"Fine," I said, relenting just to get him out of here. "Now would you just take that horrible thing out of here and go away."

He gave me another cold look. "I'm gone."

He was gone, and I was relieved. But I was also really upset. About everything.

Someone was after me, refused to let me feel safe anywhere.

And Cole seemed to hate me more now than he had before.

It was a lot to have accomplished before ten o'clock on a Saturday morning.

FOUR
Cole

Well, I'd give her this. She had balls.

Seriously, I'd butted heads with more than my share of people, and the diva certainly did a damn fine job of putting me in my place. Part of me was actually proud of her.

And part of me still wanted to strangle her.

I couldn't believe I'd actually let my guard down and didn't even think to check the damn box of muffins. Nothing should be left unchecked, and at this point, everyone was a suspect.

It wasn't until I was down in the lobby that I actually allowed myself to breathe. I couldn't slack off on this case—or any case, for that matter—but particularly this one. The sooner I got things figured out, the sooner I'd be out of here.

And away from Evangeline.

Even thinking her name had me shaking my head. It was ridiculous. Although it was kind of fun twisting it around and watching her get all pissy about it. I chuckled at the thought and realized it was the only kind of distraction I could allow myself. I was not here to play nice or socialize.

And I certainly wasn't here to get up close and personal with a client.

No matter how badly my body was saying otherwise.

"Fuck," I muttered and pulled out my phone. We had a lab in DC that we used for cases like this. There was no way

I could leave and bring it to them, and I knew they would give me shit about having to make the drive to Baltimore to pick it up.

Too bad. They got paid a lot of money to handle things like this, and I was not in the mood to play courier.

Fifteen minutes later, arrangements were made. I had gotten a kit from the trunk of my car so I could bag this stuff up and keep it protected until their guy arrived. That was one thing off my list. Now to check with the doorman. I knew Evangeline said those muffins were a normal occurrence, but I needed to know how they arrived, who delivered them, and then get with Malcolm and have him hit the bakery and question the people there.

It was a long shot, and I knew it. Chances were whoever put the mouse in there did it after the box left the bakery, but still, I had to check every angle and question every person I possibly could.

It wouldn't be so bad if I actually liked talking to people.

But I didn't.

Most people are idiots.

A fact that was confirmed once I was done with the doorman. He was completely useless. He couldn't give me an accurate description of who dropped the box off and played it off as "being busy."

Bullshit.

I realized those muffins came all the time, but Evangeline hadn't been here in this location for long, so this guy should have been paying more attention. It was an average delivery for Evangeline, not so much for the doorman. I promised the guy I was going to be talking to his boss and his boss's boss. He didn't really seem to care, but it made me feel better to issue the threat.

I was better than this.

I *knew* I was better than this, and on most cases, I would be much further along in figuring out what the hell was going on. Why couldn't I do this? Why couldn't I get a handle on where this threat was coming from? Looking at my watch, I saw I had already been away from Evangeline for almost forty-five minutes. And that was much longer than I should have allowed. Shaking my head, I walked over to the elevator and headed back up.

Once back at her apartment, I let myself in. She was nowhere in sight, and I actually breathed a sigh of relief. With her out of the way—even temporarily—I could finish making my calls. The first call was to Malcolm. I shared the morning's events with him and was glad he seemed just as perplexed as I was. With explicit directions, I sent him on his way to do some investigating on his own.

With still no sign of Evangeline, I took a minute to call Levi and chuckled at how exhausted he sounded. "What's the matter? Not getting any sleep?" I asked.

A loud yawn was the initial response followed by, "I cannot believe how much one baby can mess you up. I mean, Harper just keeps telling me he's got his days and nights mixed up, but how the hell do you fix that?"

"So were you sleeping right now?"

"I wish." Another yawn. "I doubt you're calling to check on my sleeping habits, so what's up? I thought we had a conference call planned for tomorrow."

"Yeah, I know," I said with my own weariness. "It's just… I don't know, man. I can't read this case, and it's starting to piss me off." I gave him a rundown of what I'd seen, heard, and observed and then waited for his input.

"Seems to me a large part of the issue is that there are so many possibilities. There's no obvious string of suspects because Evangeline's in such a high-profile position. Honestly, this person might not even be in Baltimore."

"No," I said adamantly. "The mouse in the muffin box says otherwise."

"Or he has an accomplice."

"Don't even say that. If I can't get a handle on one of them, how the hell am I supposed to track down two of them?"

"It's still early in the case, Cole. I know you want out of there, and I think that's part of what's messing with you. Stop thinking about the end of the case, and get your head in the here and now." He yawned loudly, and in the background I could hear the baby cry. "Listen, we'll talk again tomorrow. You're free to talk around seven in the morning, right?"

"Why don't you tell me what this is all about and save the call?"

There was a minute of hesitation. "It's really something we all need to talk about. Seb's even calling in from vacation."

"That sounds pretty serious, Levi. Come on. What's going on?"

He sighed. "I got a call yesterday. From Washington. It seems that the inquiry into what happened the day Gavin died is over."

Shit.

"The only reason I received the call is because someone majorly broke protocol to tell me. I just thought…"

He cleared his throat. "I figured we'd all discuss it now because we'll probably all be either called or summoned to the capital to talk about it."

"No fucking way. I'm not going."

"Cole..."

"No, I'm serious, man. I did my time, and I'm out. No one has any hold on me or any power over me. It's over, it's done, and I'm not talking about it ever again." I was pissed by the catch in my voice. "I can't go there again, Levi. I just can't."

"We're all feeling the same way," Levi said quietly. "Believe me, I'd like nothing more than to just move on from the whole thing. But we owe it to Gavin—and to ourselves—to see it through to the end."

"The end already fucking came! Gavin's dead! No inquiry or meeting or report is going to change that! Why are we still having to talk about it?"

In the background, the cries grew louder, and I heard Harper call out for Levi. "Look, Cole, I've got to go. Call in the morning. Please."

I told him I would, but I was still on the fence and leaning heavily toward not. But he had enough on his plate without dealing with me and my hang-ups and issues. I hung up and rested my elbows on the counter, my head in my hands.

"Are you okay?"

Great. I looked up and saw Evangeline standing beside me, concern written all over her face.

"Yeah. Why?" I asked, hating how defensive I sounded.

"I... I overheard..." She motioned toward my phone.

"Yeah, well... just... just forget that you did." I stalked away and went in search of something to drink. She stayed rooted to the spot, watching me. I wasn't really thirsty, but I needed to keep moving. I couldn't have her looking at me like that—with pity. With compassion.

"Who was Gavin?" she asked softly.

I should have put up more of a fight. I should have told her to go away.

But I didn't.

Instead, I walked over to the sofa and sat down, staring at my hands that were clasped in front of me. Before I knew it, she was sitting beside me quietly and listening intently as I pretty much bared my soul to her.

"Gavin was... my best friend. He was this amazing guy—the kind of guy who was always there for you and would do anything for you." I raked a hand through my hair. "He had the knack of looking at you and seeing you for who you really were and not... not the way everyone else did."

"He sounds like a great guy," she said quietly.

I nodded. "He was. I met him in basic training. He had joined the Marines willingly, and I sort of went as a last resort. A way to escape."

"Escape what?"

"My life." I looked over at her, and her expression hadn't really changed much. She seemed genuinely interested in what I was saying. I shrugged. "My father was the town drunk, and my mother died when I was eight. We were piss-poor, and I did what I had to do in order to survive." I was expecting to shock her, but still she didn't react. "I've stolen food, clothes, money... cars. I was into drugs while I was in high school and did my best to stay away from home. I would sometimes sleep in the alley rather than go home."

"Why?"

"Because I was the old man's punching bag when I was there. I wasn't always this big. And I used to be afraid to fight back." I gave a mirthless laugh. "I was lucky that I sort of had an overnight growth spurt. I came home one day, and the sight of me kind of took him by surprise. He punched... and I punched back."

"What did he do?"

I met her gaze and held it. "He pulled a knife on me."

"Oh my God!"

"Yeah, he pretty much was completely out of his mind—the alcohol always made him mean. He had the knife at my throat and was telling me what a worthless piece of shit I was." I shrugged again. "It wasn't new information, and he wasn't the only person in town with that opinion of me. He went on and on about what a disappointment I was, and all the while, he kept pressing the knife into my skin."

"What did you do?" she asked, leaning forward slightly.

"He may have had the knife, but his reflexes were shit. He was so busy ranting and raving and listening to the sound of his own voice that he was taken by surprise when I moved. I swung my arm out and had him on the ground with the blade at his throat. I beat him until he was unconscious."

"What happened to him?"

"At the time? I have no idea. I took the knife and all the booze in the house—along with the few belongings I had—and left." I straightened and took a deep breath. "I walked thirty miles to the next county and enlisted. I heard he died a year later."

"Oh, Cole... That's horrible."

"Why? He was a drunk. A bully. A bastard. You know how he died? He was walking the streets, drunk as a skunk, and wandered onto the train tracks. He probably never saw the damn thing coming."

Evangeline gasped.

I stood. "Believe me, no one misses him, and the world is a better place without him."

She sat silently for a long minute. "Can I ask you something?"

"Sure."

"What did you do when you found out he'd died?"

"Not a thing. The military made sure I was notified, but I was deployed overseas. There was nothing to go home for or to do."

"Did you go back after you were discharged?"

I nodded.

"But... why?"

"I had no place else to go. I found out the house was left to me, so I planned on just going back and cleaning up whatever mess the old man'd left behind and leave. It wasn't that simple because... well, I was injured and..."

"What happened to you?"

I explained to her about the explosion that had killed Gavin, my voice devoid of emotion. "Half my body was ripped apart from flying shrapnel and debris. I had broken bones. I was fairly mobile by the time I was released from the hospital, but I was far from healed. I thought I'd make a quiet reentry back into civilian life. I'd seen stories of guys like me getting a hero's welcome when they came home. Not me. All I got was a bunch of judgmental old bitches who couldn't wait to remind me of my past."

"That's not fair!" she cried.

"Yeah, I know. But it is what it is. Closed-minded people rarely change. I couldn't help my circumstances when I was a kid. Maybe if someone had bothered to pay attention to the fact that my mother was dead and my father was beating me, I wouldn't have had to steal. I might not have gotten involved with drugs. But instead, they all wanted to act as if I was just being rebellious for the sake of rebelling."

"I'm so sorry... I... I can't even imagine how that must make you feel." She reached out and took one of my hands in hers. Her skin was so soft, and when she looked up at me, her eyes were huge and filled with tears.

"Don't..." I began almost angrily. "Don't feel sorry for me. It's over. I've moved on."

"Have you? Because it doesn't seem like it. It seems like you're punishing everyone for the actions of a few people."

I tried to pull my hand away, but she held on. "I'm not a moron. I can see how people look at me."

"Do you? Do you really?"

"How do you see me, princess? The first time you looked at me, you looked your pretty little nose down at me. You looked disgusted, repulsed."

"That's not fair. You didn't give me a chance to react at all before you came out fighting. If you don't give people a chance to know you and only show them this harsh side of you, then of course they're going to look at you with disgust."

"Yeah. That's a good theory."

She looked down, and then up, and her expression had changed, as if she wasn't quite as real as she'd been the minute before. "I know this may seem like a weird question but... would you mind if I asked you some more questions about your upbringing? You know, for my character in the movie?"

If she had kicked me in the gut, it would have been less of a shock. Here I was telling her my life story and believing she's actually interested—interested in getting to know *me*—and it was all for the sake of her role in a movie?

Unable to control myself, I reached out and hauled her to her feet. Her body slammed against mine, and I got a perverse thrill from watching her wince in pain. "As a matter of fact, I do mind. Do you think this is a fucking joke? That what I just told you was for your entertainment?"

"What? No!" she cried. "I just... I thought..."

I shoved her away with disgust.

"We're done here," I muttered and walked away, not stopping until I had stormed out of the suite and slammed the door behind me.

~

By the following Friday I was ready to pull my hair out of my head.

Things had been quiet on the set—no more dead rodents or letters had arrived. I felt like a damn rent-a-cop with nothing better to do than stand around and wait.

And watch.

As much as I hated to admit it, Evangeline had some serious talent. The woman who I had essentially manhandled the previous weekend had managed to seriously impress me. She wasn't quite the diva I had originally imagined. She showed up on the set each morning without a stitch of makeup on and still managed to look beautiful.

Then she'd walk around—always with either myself or Malcolm close by—and take direction and do her scenes, and I have to tell you, some of this shit was brutal. This wasn't a glamorous role for her, and she didn't seem intimidated at all by the fact that her looks were being played down.

Maybe I had been quick to judge.

Maybe.

"She really is something, isn't she?" a quiet voice said from beside me.

I turned and saw the mousy chick, Janelle, and some guy standing next to me. I hadn't seen him before. "Hey," I said. "I'm Cole. And you are?"

"Oh, I'm Matt. Janelle and I work together. I was out with the flu for a couple of days, and today's my first day back. You're the security guy, right?"

He was the male version of Janelle. Kind of geeky, kind of mousy. The kind of guy who would blend into the background. *Hmm...*

"It's good to meet you, Matt," I forced myself to say. "Just know that Malcolm and I are working hard to make sure Evangeline's safe. We'll be checking on everything you bring to her on the set."

The kid nodded and then went back to watching the scene that was being shot. And when I turned to do the same,

I could understand why the two of them were so mesmerized. Evangeline had a lot of dialogue in this scene, and the sound of her voice was actually kind of nice.

We hadn't talked much since I stormed out of her place last weekend. The only time we did was when we were forced to and I needed to ask about her schedule or about anything or anyone that seemed out of place.

She answered in one word most of the time.

Yeah, I'd screwed up. I handled the situation like a jackass, but in my own defense, she seriously pissed me off.

Not that it was anything new, but I knew I was going to catch shit for it the next time she talked to Sebastian.

And that was another thing that had me on edge this week. I'd called in for the conference call and basically, sometime in the near future, we were all going to be called to DC to wrap up the report.

The conversation was oddly quiet. Levi talked but seemed distracted, and none of us had much to say. I knew why— They all blamed me. What else was there to say? We were going to go listen to some official reading of a report, and although no charges were likely to be filed, it was going to be out there—voiced loud and clear—my poor judgment cost Gavin his life.

Like I needed anyone to tell that to me.

I looked down at my watch and saw that it was almost seven. The shooting was going late today, but according to the schedule I was given, they were expected to finish up around nine. They had some scenes in the alley that required being shot at night. After that, Evangeline wasn't going to be needed on the set for about four days.

Only... no one else knew that. I had talked to Pete, the director, and a fake schedule had been handed out to the rest of the cast and crew. We were going to try to see if we could catch anyone off guard. So Malcolm and his guys were going to come here and follow the same routine they had every day since filming began, and I was taking Evangeline out of town for a few days.

The plan was to secretly whisk her away but keep a decoy car and crew hanging out here to keep an eye on things.

With any luck, our stalker would make a move. Or a mistake.

And I'd be able to wrap this case up by the end of next week.

FIVE
Evangeline

Things were better when I was actually on set.

At least then I had plenty to distract me from Cole and his constant, brooding presence.

But yesterday evening, after I'd finished on set, we left Baltimore to go to an upscale DC hotel that guaranteed absolute privacy—a kind of makeshift safe house we could stay in for the next few days, when I wasn't needed on set. Cole had some sort of plan to entrap the stalker to reveal himself by giving the cast and crew a false schedule for me. He thought it would be an efficient way to catch the guy quickly so this whole ordeal wouldn't have to drag on.

I was pretty sure he was just as anxious about getting this job done so he could be rid of me as I was excited to be rid of him.

It was very stressful to have him hanging around all the time—since he consumed my whole mind, especially when I was off set and had nothing else to do.

I was pretty sure the next few days were going to be hellish for both of us.

I slept in later than normal the next morning after we had arrived at the hotel suite, because I spent most of the night tossing and turning and thinking in turn about the stalker and Cole. It was almost ten by the time I came out of the bedroom.

I wasn't surprised to see that Cole was there, awake, sitting on one of the stools at the kitchen bar, drinking coffee and doing something on his phone.

He glanced up, and his gray eyes went briefly hot when he saw me.

At least that was what I thought his expression meant as his eyes ran up and down my body. I was wearing a camisole and little knit shorts—which is what I'd slept in—and I hadn't bothered to brush my hair or wash my face.

I felt a little jump of excitement at the idea that he was attracted to me. Sure, it wasn't that unusual—since I had a pretty good body and I had a kind of sex-kitten thing going with my public persona. And Cole was obviously a normal man who was likely to appreciate a somewhat decent female body. But I couldn't help but feel like he was too cool and competent to let himself react to any attraction he felt for me unless he was *very* attracted.

And I liked the idea of his being *very* attracted to me since I was more attracted to the arrogant ass every day.

"Good morning," I said, managing not to leer at him, despite how sexy and masculine he looked in his T-shirt, which set off his tight shoulders, and his jeans, which looked great on his long legs and tight butt.

"Morning."

We'd been pretty cool with each other for the past week, ever since he was such a jerk after I'd asked him about his background. We were occasionally snippy, but mostly we just circled each other, feigning politeness with absolutely no warmth.

I was used to getting along with most people, so the tension was very uncomfortable for me.

I went to the coffeepot and reminded myself that this would be over soon. Hopefully, Cole's plan would work so the whole thing would be done by the end of the week.

"How did you sleep?" The mild question wasn't friendly in any way, but it felt like a peace offering, just the same.

"Not too well," I said, watching the coffee stream into my mug. "What about you?"

He didn't answer, so I glanced back over my shoulder. He was giving a half shrug.

"Did you sleep at all?" I asked, as it occurred to me that I'd never seen him sleep—or even seen him go into a bedroom for the night.

I was still looking back at him, so I saw the second half shrug.

"You can't stay awake all the time," I said, sipping my coffee and watching his controlled face.

"I sleep when I need to. I've gotten used to going without."

"It can't be good for you though."

"I do a lot of things that aren't good for me."

I could well believe that. He was in great shape, but I was sure it was because he was so active and not because he took really good care of himself. He seemed more like the kind of guy who lived hard and whose body had hardened accordingly.

"But still—" I began.

"You were just telling me you didn't get much sleep, so you're hardly a model of healthy living."

As always, his dry tone only served to rile me up. "Well, these are unusual circumstances for me. I went to bed at a reasonable time, but everything going on makes me too nervous to sleep. I usually get plenty of sleep. And I try to eat mostly healthy, and I do yoga, and I don't binge drink or anything. I guarantee I'm healthier than you."

There was no good reason for me to feel so defensive, except it always felt like he was judging and attacking me.

"Yeah, right. Getting so high you dance half-naked on a table in a nightclub is healthy."

I stiffened, realizing he'd seen that notorious video of me from when I'd been nineteen.

I hated that video—taken on someone's phone—and I'd never be able to live it down.

I'd gone a little wild that year, trying to shake my child star reputation. I'd done some stupid things. But that video made it look a lot worse than it really was, and it had been shown all over the news and internet.

I controlled my reaction—made up of anger and something like betrayal—and narrowed my eyes at him. "It was one night. It happened to be documented. Are you really going to tell me you've never had a night that would look just as bad if it had been caught on camera?"

He met my eyes for a minute, and there was momentarily something like understanding in his gaze. Then he glanced away and muttered, "I've had hundreds of those nights."

The words actually made me feel better.

How we'd gotten into this conversation, I didn't know. We'd just been talking about how we'd slept the night before. But it was the best conversation we'd had in a week. He felt like a human again—and not some cold, sexy stranger.

I let out a breath. "Everyone has."

He turned his head to meet my gaze again, as if in response to the softness in my tone. Our backgrounds might have been light-years apart, but we still understood each other. Knew each other somehow. Were similar in ways neither one of us could have predicted.

"Not everyone," he said in a different tone, with almost a smile on his mobile mouth. "You should meet my buddy's girlfriend, Kristin. I don't think she's had a wild night in her life."

I laughed. "Maybe she's had nights you don't know about."

"Maybe. But I doubt it."

"Don't you like her?"

"Sure. She's great. I'm just not sure what she sees in Declan since he had nothing but wild nights until he met her."

"Well, love changes people. And sometimes we're drawn to people who are completely opposite from us." I'd come over to sit on a stool beside him as we talked, but I flushed a little as I realized what I'd just said.

It was true. It was absolutely true—since Cole was as different from me as possible, and I was ridiculously drawn to him—but I didn't mean to say it. What if he thought I was talking about us?

He didn't react to the words. Just gave another half shrug. "Yeah. I suppose that's what it is. They're happy, so why should I question it? It's all a mystery to me anyway."

"What is?"

"Love. The way people couple up. It never makes sense, it always comes out of the blue, and I never expect it to last."

I'd always felt the same way—like love was some sort of magic that happened to everyone but me. I'd sometimes watch couples and wonder in bewilderment how they'd gotten together and what they saw in each other and why something like that had never happened to me.

I'd dated plenty, but I didn't think I'd ever really been in love. Whenever I dated someone, even if I really liked him, it always felt like I was going through the motions, like I was pretending to be someone other than me.

I couldn't imagine what it was like to be with someone for real and just be me.

"Yeah," I said at last, looking away from him since I suddenly wanted to reach out and touch him. "I've never gotten it either."

We sat side by side, drinking coffee, lost in our own thoughts. But it felt like we were bonding somehow.

When I was feeling too vulnerable, I realized I needed to start thinking about something else. "So what are we going to do today?"

"Just hang out here, if it's all right with you. I'd rather you not go out since you might be recognized, and then the news might get out about where you are."

"Okay," I said, realizing he was right, and it would be better to just catch this stalker as quickly as possible. I wasn't thrilled about being cooped up, but at least I felt safe here—in this anonymous, impersonal hotel suite. With Cole.

"Malcom will report in if anything unusual happens on the set."

"Okay. You'll let me know if you learn anything?"

"Of course."

I nodded and let out a long breath. The stalker must be in Baltimore, which felt very far away from me now. If nothing else, at least I'd have a break from the constant fear for a few days.

I'd take whatever I could get.

On that thought, Cole's phone rang. He glanced at it and picked up. "Yeah." After a minute, he said, "Okay. Bring it up."

"What is it?" I demanded, when he hung up.

"Delivery."

"What?" I jumped to my feet. "No one knows I'm here. I shouldn't be getting a delivery."

"It's from—"

I suddenly felt naked, completely vulnerable, as if there was nowhere in the world I could be safe. I kept reliving that sickening moment of finding the mouse in with the muffins. "How did he find me? How could he possibly find me here?" My voice grew shrill on the last words.

Cole reached out to hold my upper arms. "Evangeline, calm down."

I tried to shake off his strong hands. "I'm not going to calm down. How the hell did the stalker find me here? Who is doing this to me?"

One little part of my mind recognized I was overreacting, but I simply couldn't help it. I'd been feeling safe just a minute ago, but now it was all blown away.

Cole wouldn't let go of me. "Evangeline, stop," he said, his voice low and slightly hoarse. "Stop. It's from Sebastian. It's from *Sebastian*."

The words finally broke through my panicked brain, and I froze, trying to process what he'd just said. "What?"

"The delivery is from Sebastian. He was just trying to be nice. It's not the stalker."

I was shaking helplessly as I finally understood what he was telling me.

"It's not the stalker," he said again as a knock sounded on the door.

The noise made me jump, and Cole's fingers were still wrapped around my upper arms.

"Are you okay?" he asked, looking tense and concerned.

I nodded mutely.

"Can I get the door?"

I nodded again, unable to say anything.

Shit. I was an idiot. A fool. A silly, embarrassing nervous wreck. There was no justification for my breakdown, and I couldn't believe I'd actually reacted that way.

I wasn't normally so melodramatic and ridiculous.

Cole let go of me at last and walked to the door, where he accepted a potted orchid from the hotel staff member who'd carried it up.

It was a beautiful plant—a lovely, exotic violet color—but I stared at it suspiciously. "It's really from Sebastian?" I managed to ask.

Cole nodded. "He said he was sending it over." He put the orchid down, carefully inspecting the plant and the card and even the soil it was planted in.

"It's okay?" I asked, forcing myself to step over, even though I was still shaking.

"It's fine, Evangeline," Cole murmured. He put an arm around my shoulders, pulling me against him in a comforting gesture. "I promise it's fine. The stalker hasn't found you."

I nodded, staring down at the lovely, delicate blooms. It was really nice of Sebastian. He was trying to be a friend, make me feel better.

And I jumped to the conclusion that it was an attack.

What the hell was wrong with me?

"Shit, princess," Cole said hoarsely, pulling me into a full hug. "It's okay. It's really okay."

For some reason his obvious concern and the tenderness in his touch and voice completely broke me. I shook against him in silent sobs—not really crying but feeling completely broken.

I wasn't much of a crier under normal circumstances. I had no idea what was happening to me.

Cole's arms were tight and strong and protective, and they felt better than anything in the world. He wasn't saying anything now, but he didn't need to.

He was trying to make me feel better.

He did.

After a minute, I was able to control myself and straighten up. His arms loosened but not all the way. He gazed down at me, something soft and intense in his expression. "Are you okay?" he asked.

"Yeah." I sniffed a little, although there were only a few tears. "I'm sorry about that. I have no idea what happened."

"You were scared."

"Yeah, but there was no reason for it. It was the epitome of an overreaction."

"It's normal," he said. "You've been a trooper this whole time, but the stress and fear eventually catches up to you. It doesn't matter how much protection you have. The threat of a stalker always does that. It keeps you from ever feeling safe."

I nodded, feeling understood and much less stupid. "It's been nothing but little things, but…"

"They add up. He wants you to feel this way."

I took a few deep breaths, flattening my hands on Cole's firm chest.

"I'm going to catch him. I promise." His eyes were still intense and protective, but now they were something more, something hot.

I suddenly felt hot too, and I slid my hands up toward his shoulders. "Thank you," I whispered, leaning toward him.

I wanted nothing in the world more than to touch him, kiss him, be with him in every way.

I knew he wanted it too. It was clear in his eyes, in his touch, in the way his hand slid up toward the back of my head.

But then he suddenly dropped his hands, and I realized what was about to happen.

I ducked my head, my heart racing and my body shaking again—this time for an entirely different reason.

Cole was so tense he was frozen, and I could see from a quick glance that he was aroused. It was strangely exciting but also terrifying.

I wasn't sure what I would have done, but I didn't have the chance. Cole gave himself a quick shake and said, "If you're all right, I'm going to call in and get a report from Baltimore."

I knew the words were intended to put us back into a professional dynamic, and they worked. Kissing Cole would have been a huge mistake—for both of us—so it was just as well to get some distance.

"Yeah," I said, steadying my breath. "I'm fine."

He walked out of the room quickly, a little stiffly—probably just to stand outside the door in the hall—and I tried to shake off the intensity of the moment before.

That was easier said than done though. I kept thinking about it for the rest of the day.

∼

Cole kept his distance for most of the morning and afternoon, but he finally loosened up again after I had ordered room service for dinner and invited him to have some.

I didn't want him to think I was angry or awkward about our moment. I'd much prefer for him to believe it was no big deal to me at all. So I made a point of being friendly with him and asking him to join me for dinner.

He did, and we had a conversation about his time in the Marines. I asked him some about his upbringing, but he evidently didn't want to talk about that.

That was my fault. I never should have said I wanted to hear more about his childhood for research purposes. It hadn't been true even then—I'd just gotten scared about how close I felt to him and had to do something to cover it—but I realized he wasn't going to forget it.

As we were finishing up, I said, "I guess I should do some work this evening." I hadn't done much of anything all day, and I was starting to feel guilty about it—since this movie was important to my career.

"What work?" he asked.

"Go over a few of my scenes," I explained. "There are a few I'm not sure I've really got yet."

"Okay," he said, looking interested. "Do you just read them out loud then?"

"Yeah, although usually Cali reads them with me since it's kind of hard by myself."

Then I had an idea. "Maybe you can go over them with me," I suggested, almost smiling at the reaction I imagined he'd have to this idea.

I wasn't disappointed. His mouth dropped open. "What?"

"Maybe you can do the scenes with me. Just read the lines for the other characters so I have someone to respond to."

"You've got to be kidding me."

"Well, why not? You're not doing anything but hanging out here this evening. How hard can it be to read a few lines?"

"I'm no actor."

"Don't act. Just read. Please?" I gave him an over-the-top, beseeching look, knowing instinctively that teasing him into it would be more effective than trying to make a rational argument to get him to agree to the proposal.

He rolled his eyes.

"Pretty please," I cooed. "It won't take very long. And the quicker I can get a handle on the scenes, the quicker the filming can take place, and the quicker we can wrap things up."

The logic of this plea was rather shaky, but I was batting my eyelashes very prettily, so I didn't think it would matter.

He obviously knew what I was trying to do, and he rolled his eyes again, muttering under his breath. But he said, "Fine. I'll stand here and read lines. But don't expect anything else."

"Thank you!" I jumped up to grab the script, turning to the first scene I needed to work on. It was a good one since there was just one other character in it.

I explained the context and his character, and then Cole stood in the middle of the living area and started to read.

At first he just read the words blankly, with no inflection or intonation. I did my best with my own lines, but I was very distracted by him standing there with the script in his hand, and I had trouble not giggling over his delivery.

As the scene went on, though, he got more into it—especially when it turned into an argument between my character and her romantic interest. By the end of the scene, he was doing a pretty decent job, so I gave him appropriate compliments when the scene was done and asked if we could do it again.

He agreed with a bad-tempered expression, but I knew he wasn't really reluctant.

"Try to give it a little more spirit," I suggested, mostly just to tease him.

He glared at me and read his first line.

At first I thought he was heeding my advice since his lines were much more dramatic than they'd been the first time. But then I realized he was just being contrary. His delivery became more and more over the top until it was a farce of a genuine performance.

I was a little annoyed to begin with, since it was impossible for me to really practice in response to such melodrama. But eventually his over-the-top dramatics started to tickle me. I tried to hold back my amusement—since it would signal a victory for him—but I just couldn't do it.

By the end of the scene, I couldn't even say my lines since I was suppressing so much laughter.

He kept a straight face the whole time, but I could see he was pleased. His gray eyes reflected a kind of genuine pleasure I'd never seen there before.

"How was that?" he asked when I gasped out the final line of the scene.

"You know exactly how it was," I said, trying once again—unsuccessfully—to keep from giggling. "You botched the whole scene on purpose."

"I was going for a heartfelt performance."

"If that was a heartfelt performance for you, I'd hate to see you when you get riled up and lose control."

The words were supposed to be dry and aloof, but they didn't quite work. Even as I said them, I had very wrong thoughts about how he might lose control.

He evidently had the same wrong thoughts because his expression flared with sexual heat that left me breathless.

But he turned away almost immediately, as I should have expected, and I decided I might as well go to bed because nothing more exciting was likely to happen tonight.

∼

Four hours later, I woke with a start from a deep sleep when I heard an alarm blaring.

I had no idea what it was as I sat up straight in bed, my heartbeat and my breath both caught in my throat.

I managed to process that I was in a hotel suite, but I had no idea what the loud, grating sound might be. I even reached for the clock next to the bed, but hitting it with my hand did nothing to stop the sound.

Then Cole burst into the bedroom, dressed in a pair of jeans and no shirt.

"What is it?" I asked, barely able to speak over the lump of fear in my throat.

"Fire alarm. I called and it's not a planned drill, so we need to go down."

"Is there a fire?"

"I don't know. It could just be something burning or a short in the electrical, but we can't risk it. Get up."

He looked urgent, and it made me even more nervous.

I certainly didn't want to burn to death in a hotel fire, but the threat of fire seemed pretty distant. Under normal circumstances, I'd exit by the emergency stairs without a second thought.

But these weren't normal circumstances. What if the stalker had found me? What if the stalker was responsible for the fire alarm? What if this was some elaborate ruse to get to me?

I would have thought the fears were silly, but I could see similar thoughts in Cole's tense expression.

I grabbed for a hoodie and slipped on shoes as he hurried me out of the bedroom since I was wearing nothing but a short, sleeveless nightgown.

If nothing else, I didn't want a picture of me in my lingerie to show up in the gossip columns tomorrow morning.

There were two men waiting in the hall when we left the suite, and I realized they must be hotel security. They walked down with us to the emergency stairs from this floor, which were separated from the main emergency stairs that most of the hotel guests used.

The hotel was designed to house very important clientele. I was pretty far down on the list, but I must be among the most important staying tonight.

Cole took my hand as we walked quickly down the stairs. It was probably just to make sure I didn't dawdle, but it felt protective, almost intimate.

We were on the twenty-eighth floor, so it was a long journey down, with the alarms blaring the whole time.

When we got down and burst out of the building into the night, I shrunk back as I realized we weren't far from the crowd of other hotel guests. But before I could feel vulnerable, a car drove up directly in front of us, and Cole pushed me into the back seat.

It was very nicely done, and we were driving away from the hotel before anything could happen—even before someone could recognize me and click my picture.

Cole got on the phone immediately, trying to figure out what was happening. We drove around for a while until it became clear the fire alarm was caused by a small fire in the kitchen that had generated enough smoke to set off the alarms throughout the hotel.

So it was just a fluke, I realized. Unfortunate but just one of those things.

Not about me at all.

I was relieved. Of course I was relieved. But I also felt weird and shaky and uncertain since it had all happened so fast, and I was having trouble keeping up.

We waited about thirty minutes after the firefighters gave the all clear, and the other guests were allowed to return to their rooms before we returned ourselves. It was after two in the morning, and the hotel was dead quiet.

We took the private elevator up to my floor, and I went right to my bedroom.

Cole was on the phone again, so I pulled the covers up over me and tried to calm down.

I wasn't in danger. Everything was fine. I was as safe as I was going to be.

I just couldn't stop trembling.

A few minutes later, he walked into the bedroom without knocking, and I sat up abruptly in bed, surprised by his appearance but kind of glad to see him.

He looked strong and solid and safe, and I liked having him near me.

I had no idea when that had happened.

"Sorry," he muttered, pausing. "I didn't realize you'd already be in bed."

"Is everything okay?"

"Yeah. Everything's fine. None of this had anything to do with you." He walked over closer to the bed, studying my face. The lights were off in the room, but light streamed in from the living area.

"Good."

"Are you okay?" he asked, standing right next to the bed.

"Yeah." I didn't feel okay. I felt like my heart was going to explode in my chest.

He reached out to cup my face. "You don't look okay. You're shaking."

"I'm fine. I don't know why I can't stop trembling." I hugged myself. "It just all happened so fast. I was... I was..."

"Scared."

"Yeah. I thought it might be..." I trailed off, not wanting to say the words.

"Me too." He sat down on the edge of the bed, stroking his hand back into my hair. "But it's okay now. It wasn't what we thought."

"Good." His hand felt good against my cheek, against my hair, and I tried to lean into it. "Thank you, by the way. You handled it all really... really..."

"Really what?" His voice was strangely hushed.

"Really well."

"Good." His eyes were devouring my face. "So do you think you can stop trembling now?"

"I'm trying." I really was, but if anything, I was trembling more now than I'd been before—not just from fear anymore, but from rising excitement.

His eyes continued to scan my face and it wasn't enough. I wanted—needed—his touch.

Swallowing hard, I leaned in a little closer and gently licked my lips. I met his gaze. "I...I might need something to help me...relax."

He leaned toward me until his mouth was just a breath away from mine. "What would help?"

I knew exactly what would help, and I wanted it so much I was reaching toward him. "You know what would help. Stop being so stubborn."

"Shit, princess," he muttered, his expression blazing hot for just a second before he took my head in both his hands to kiss me.

I moaned softly in pleasure as his lips started to move against mine. They were gentle for just a moment before they became hungry and seeking. I opened to his urgency and wound my arms around his neck, pressing my breasts against his chest, which was still bare. He'd never taken the time to put a shirt on.

His arm moved around my body, tightening almost painfully as he became more passionate. My own lips and body were eager—almost embarrassingly so—but I couldn't even care. I couldn't remember ever wanting anyone so much.

The kiss deepened until my nipples had tightened and arousal pulsed between my legs. I could feel he was turned on too, and I tried to rub myself against him but was frustrated by our awkward position.

I was about to make things easier by crawling into his lap when he suddenly broke the kiss.

It was almost painful to be completely drowning in the embrace and then suddenly have it torn away from me. He jerked to his feet, flushed, aroused, and tenser than I'd ever seen him.

I had no idea what he would say as he stared down at me, but I was sure I didn't want to hear it.

SIX
Cole

I left.

The last time I'd felt this kind of panic—this overwhelming need to flee—was when I left home after nearly beating my old man to death.

I should know better.

I *do* know better.

You don't get involved with a client.

I mean, sure, Levi, Sebastian, *and* Declan had all pretty much disregarded that basic rule of business, but I wasn't weak like they were. I was here to do a job, and sleeping with Evangeline wasn't part of that.

No matter how much my hard-on said otherwise.

It was a moment of weakness. Nothing more, nothing less. And it sure as hell wasn't any big deal. *She* was not a big deal.

I'd been with a lot of women since getting out of the service, so it wasn't like I was hard up for female company. Hell, I could walk out of this damn hotel and have someone soft and curvy ready to spend the night with me within an hour.

Unfortunately, I didn't want that. Okay, not a big deal. I was a grown man, and I could deal with… whatever the hell this was. Fascination. Proximity. Lust. Whatever it was, I needed to just catch my breath and get my head back on straight and focus on the task at hand.

Stalker.

Threats.

Evangeline.

Shit. I could only distance myself from her so much. She was the reason I was here. She was the reason I was ready to pull my hair out of my damn head. It was fucking frustrating is what it was.

I paced up and down the hallway, checked the stairwell and the utility closets. I even managed to grab a few minutes talking to one of the staff walking around delivering room service to another suite. But I could only stay out here for so long. Eventually I was going to have to go back inside and face the music.

Not looking forward to that. I mean, what the hell was I supposed to say? *"Um… hey, sorry I pounced. But you were kind of asking me to and I'm horny."* Yeah. Like that would go over well.

I was so screwed.

I started to walk back to the suite when a thought came to mind. I knew my motivation for kissing Evangeline, but… what was her deal? She was this posh, sophisticated actress. She was rich and pampered and had a history of dating the latest pretty boys in Hollywood. So what the hell was she doing begging me to kiss her?

Was I more research for her role?

Was she just slumming it?

Passing the time?

I didn't like any of those options. But just the thought of them had the desired effect. I no longer wanted to go back inside and kiss her again. I wanted answers. I wanted to know what her deal was and to tell her to quit playing games.

And then I realized I was actually disappointed. For a brief moment back there, I actually let my guard down—*again*—and let myself think that I was… worthy. That I was someone a rich girl like Evangeline could actually want. But I was kidding myself. It was never gonna happen. I'd never be good enough.

I almost laughed out loud at the image that popped into my head—me at some movie premiere with Evangeline. Right. Like she'd ever want to be seen out in public with me. I could just hear the questions now: *"Hey, Evangeline, last year you bought Oscar-nominee Brett Reynolds with you and now you're with…? Where'd you two meet?"* And then she'd cringe and probably act as if I wasn't actually with her, just to avoid the truth. Because that wouldn't be pretty. *"Oh, Cole's from the bad side of Baltimore. I think he almost killed his father—but he did kill his best friend! I thought it would be fun to make him play dress-up and maybe make him feel like he's worthy for a night. Sweet, right?"*

And we were back to being pissed.

I stormed back into the suite ready for battle, but the lights were almost all off and Evangeline's bedroom door was shut.

Dammit.

It looked like our little talk would have to wait until morning.

~

"Excuse me," she asked sleepily the next morning.

"You heard me," I said with a snap in my voice. "What's your deal?"

"I... I don't know what you're talking about." Confusion was written all over her face, but I couldn't be sure if she was genuinely confused or still half asleep.

I leaned in close to be certain I'd be heard. "What was that all about last night? Were you interested in just... slumming it for a bit to pass the time? Or were you hoping to add a little something to your resume to help with your current movie role?"

"You son of a—" She raised a hand, like she was thinking of slapping me, but I caught her wrist. Her eyes blazed with fire.

"Watch yourself, princess, and just answer the fucking question."

For a long minute she simply glared at me. Then she yanked her wrist from my grasp and took a step back. "I can't *believe* you'd accuse me of something like that."

I snorted with disbelief. "I believe we've been over this quite a few times. I know you don't like me. I know you think I'm not competent or worthy of being around you, so why don't you save us all the wounded-little-girl act. Save it for a scene."

"Bastard," she spat before turning to get herself a cup of coffee.

"Sweetheart, I never pretended to be anything else. You can call me all the names you want if it makes you feel better. I don't really give a shit. But take your games and play them with someone else. I'm not interested, and I certainly don't have the time. I'm here to figure out who is making those threats to you."

"Then maybe you should do that and quit mauling me," she snapped before slamming a cabinet door shut.

"You'll know when you've been mauled, *Evalynn*," I said, just to be snarky. In an instant I knew the barb hit its mark. Her spine stiffened, and her eyes momentarily went wide. "Maybe you need to speak to a therapist," I went on casually. "You know, maybe you've got that whole transference thing going on—you know, looking at me with hero worship or something because I'm here taking care of you."

Evangeline slammed her mug down on the counter and took a step toward me. "You arrogant son of a bitch! There is *nothing* heroic about you. You haven't done shit since you've been on this case. When we get back to the set, I'm calling Sebastian and asking for someone else to handle the case." She stopped and took a breath. "You were right. I do think you're incompetent. And on top of that, you're nothing but a pain in the ass."

And she stomped away.

I waited until I heard her door slam shut.

"Sticks and stones, princess. Sticks and stones."

~

She was going to be the death of me.

We'd been back on set for two days, and Evangeline had taken every opportunity to fuck with every single plan I'd put into place. She never did call Sebastian. Obviously, she decided that doing everything humanly possible to make me look like a jackass was the better way to go.

She may not have had to worry about the threat of a stalker for much longer because I may strangle her myself.

Prison would totally be worth it.

Yesterday she convinced Malcolm's guys to let her go shopping. *Shopping!* I was meeting with the head of the studio and the producers and directors, and apparently, she managed to convince Malcolm's men that I gave clearance for her to go to the mall.

By the time I'd gotten out of the meeting and realized what had happened, I had pretty much reamed everyone within earshot for their incompetence. I damn near made Malcolm cry, and the last time I saw Matt and Janelle, they were hiding under a lunch table. When I had caught up with her and her entourage parading through Saks Fifth Avenue, she had about a dozen photographers around her along with fifty or so adoring fans. She had the nerve to look smug.

Back in the town car, I screamed until I thought I would burst a vessel and told her how her little stunt was beyond stupid. It was childish and reckless. She seemed contrite.

"I know I should have cleared it with you first," she said, "but I had protection with me. I can't just sit around waiting for something to happen. I refuse to give this… this person that much control over me."

I actually believed her. Hell, I even sympathized with her.

Clearly she was a better actress than I gave her credit for. Why? Because twenty-four hours later and she was by the gate posing for more pictures and was only a step away from making it some sort of press conference.

Maybe I should offer to paint a bull's-eye on her and save the stalker some time.

Clearly Malcolm's guys didn't understand the severity of what was going on. I would have thought after everything that happened yesterday that they'd get it.

But I was wrong.

She managed this little stunt by taking advantage of the five minutes I was off meeting with Malcolm and the director about tomorrow's shoot. The guy guarding the door was fairly new to all this, and she managed to sweet-talk him into believing she held court with her fans every day for a few minutes.

Like she was the fucking queen.

Now I was stuck stalking across the lot and having to pull her away from the crowd without looking like I was pulling her away.

"Maybe it would be better if I asked her," Malcolm said as he walked beside me, clearly reading my mind.

"Why?"

He shrugged. "She's obviously pissed at you for something, and I wouldn't put it past her to make a bit of a scene just so she could embarrass you."

The growl of frustration escaped before I could even stop it.

"What did you do to rile her up?" Malcolm asked. It was an innocent enough question. I just couldn't give him an honest answer. "I thought the two of you were finally on the same page."

"Yeah, well... we were. Until she didn't get her way." It wasn't a total lie. And it seemed to shut Malcolm up for the time being. We were about a dozen feet from Evangeline. She hadn't spotted us yet. "I'm going to step aside so she doesn't see me. Go over and tell her it's time to go."

Malcolm nodded.

"Oh... and Malcolm?" I said before he stepped away.

"Yeah?"

"Fire that guy."

He didn't argue. He simply nodded and started toward Evangeline.

I moved and stood back and watched. She smiled brightly at Malcolm as soon as she spotted him. I knew the moment he spoke, even though Malcolm's back was to me, because Evangeline's face went from pleasant to guarded to pissed. She immediately began looking around for me, but I stayed in the shadows.

It took five minutes, but Malcolm finally had her on the move and walking toward our town car—which was now in a different location. I was behind them when I heard her questioning where they were going, and if I wasn't mistaken, she almost sounded nervous.

"Thanks to your theatrics, Ellie May, we had to mix things up a bit. Tonight the car is picking us up back here."

She spun and glared at me. "But... I need to go to the trailer and get..."

"Too bad." I interrupted. "You should have thought of that before you decided to flirt your way into making the guard believe you gave photo ops on a daily basis. You've cost us enough time, and you've cost that guy his job. Tell

Malcolm what you need, and if he has time, he'll bring it to the apartment. Otherwise, deal without it."

"I despise you."

I ignored her words and placed my hand on her arm where Malcolm's had just been and helped her—none too gently—into the car. "Good. Remember that feeling for tomorrow's shoot. I hear it's an emotional scene."

She had the good sense to snap her pretty little mouth closed without saying another word. I slammed the door and quickly sprinted around to the other side. "Go and secure her trailer, Mal. If you see anything you really think she needs, bring it over. Otherwise, go home for the night. Hopefully, tomorrow will be a little less eventful."

He nodded and walked away, and I climbed into the car beside her and motioned for the driver to go. The guy knew the drill. Every night he took a different route back to the apartment. It wasn't a great plan, but we also hadn't spotted anyone following us either.

"If you pull another stunt again tomorrow, I'll make sure you're pulled from this movie," I said matter-of-factly.

Evangeline gasped. "You can't do that."

I turned and faced her, my expression neutral. "I can and I will. If you insist on courting danger—"

"I had a guard with me." She interrupted.

That was true—she hadn't done anything that was genuinely foolish except not let me keep her as safe as I wanted—but that was irrelevant to me at the moment. "If you insist on being reckless, they'll cut you loose. You'll become a liability to them. If you get hurt on their time, on their set? They'll be responsible."

Her mouth moved to speak, but no words came out. Then she finally looked out the window and muttered, "I should have called Sebastian."

"Yup. You should have." I waited before adding, "Why didn't you?"

"Because making you miserable was more fun," she said begrudgingly.

"Yeah. Look how that worked out for you." And then it hit me. She was getting back at me for what had happened—for rejecting her. "What's the matter, princess? No one ever reject you before?"

Her head snapped around, her eyes wide with disbelief. "Excuse me?"

"I guess all those pretty Hollywood types never tell you no." I shrugged. "You shouldn't take it personally. You're just not my type."

"You are unbelievable, you know that? I cannot *believe* the size of your ego! You think I did all those things because of a kiss?"

I shrugged again. "You know the saying... If it walks like a duck."

She rolled her eyes and threw up her hands in disgust. "Unreal. Un-freaking real."

Unable to help myself, I leaned in close. Big mistake. Her perfume hit me hard, and everything in me ached to reach out and touch her, to breathe her in. I shook my head to clear it and focus. "I think you're pissed because I'm not like the men you normally have around you. I'm not tripping over myself to be with you. I'm not panting after you. I was able to walk away from you."

Before she could respond, we pulled up in front of her building. Luckily, she remembered the drill—she was not to get out of the car without me being there to open the door. I climbed out and took a minute to just take a couple of deep breaths.

In. Out. In. Out.

"Keep it together," I muttered and walked around to her side of the car and pulled the door open.

Doing her best to ignore me, Evangeline stood and stepped aside while I closed the door. We walked to the entrance of the building where the doorman held the door for us and wished us a good evening. Ever since his little *faux pas* with the muffins, he'd been exceptionally attentive.

Too little, too late, but whatever.

We rode up in the elevator in silence.

At the door to her apartment, I unlocked it and let us in. She stood to the right of the inside of the door while I did a quick sweep of the apartment. "Clear," I said and then watched as she stalked across the living room toward her bedroom. The loud slam of the door told me we weren't going to be talking anymore tonight.

Fine. By. Me.

I was keyed up and paced the space. I was still fucking clueless. There was nothing out of place. There was no one around who shouldn't be, and those who were, were quickly being eliminated as suspects. I was stumped. I couldn't figure out where this threat was coming from.

All I knew was that we seemed to be doing a better job at keeping people at bay. No more weird deliveries, and nothing had shown up either here or at the set for over a week. While that was good news in and of itself, it didn't help us with figuring out who our suspect was.

Pouring myself a drink, I sat down on the sofa and rested my head back. I was exhausted. Mentally and physically. It had never taken this long. I was good at what I did, and for the first time ever, I couldn't get a read on a situation.

I could hear drawers slamming and Evangeline muttering and cursing under her breath. Yeah, she was pissed. Message received. Well, newsflash, so was I. The difference between the two of us was that I was going to sit here and keep it all in my head while she obviously felt the need to have a temper tantrum.

I knew she was immature.

Maybe if I kept saying things like that enough I'd be able to believe them. The truth of the matter was that I had a lot of respect for Evangeline. I didn't want to, but I did. She'd pretty much held it together during all this, and other than the past two days, she'd followed all our instructions without really complaining.

She was talented. I mean seriously talented. Sometimes when they were filming, I just stood back and watched her and just… man. There weren't any words. I listened to her and watched, and for a time I was able to forget that I was watching an actress perform. She transformed, and her talent was just staggering.

And she was beautiful. So beautiful she made me ache. Never in my life had I seen a woman like her. I knew she was beautiful, but I thought—mistakenly—Evangeline looked the way she did with the help of a team of makeup artists.

I was wrong.

Being that I was essentially living with her for weeks now, I'd seen her at every hour of the day, with makeup and without, and if I was being honest, I thought she looked better without all the war paint on. Her skin was flawless, and from the one time I'd actually allowed myself to touch it, it was as smooth and soft as silk.

My fingers began to twitch at just the thought of touching her skin again.

And not just the skin on her face.

I wanted to touch all of her. And it was getting harder and harder not to.

She was bewitching, and I should have known better. I'd only be making a fool out of myself to actually believe that someone like her could be attracted to someone like me, but that didn't seem to stop me from wanting it to be true.

I was pathetic.

Once this case was over, I'd be just like thousands of guys all over the world— I'd jackoff to her picture too. The only difference was that I'd at least have the memory of what it was like to actually hold her in my arms and touch her and kiss her.

Even if it was for only a minute.

See? Pathetic.

I quickly finished my drink and stood and stretched. It had been a bitch of a day, and really, I needed some sleep. When this case was over, I was going to take a month off and just fucking sleep. By that time, I would definitely deserve it.

Making my rounds, I made sure the entire apartment was secure. Off in the distance I heard another door slam. She was going to take a shower. It was part of her routine, and I was used to it. And I tried not to imagine her standing naked with water cascading down her body.

I didn't succeed.

Doors locked? Check. Windows locked and blinds closed? Check. I turned off the lights in the entryway, kitchen, and living room, and because I was a glutton for punishment, I checked the door to Evangeline's bedroom.

Locked.

Fucking check.

I sighed and walked to my own room and flipped on the light as I kicked off my shoes. Sleep. I needed some sleep. Tossing my shirt on the chair in the corner, I sat on the side of the bed, raked a hand through my hair, and contemplated how long I was going to let myself sleep tonight. I'd love to give myself a solid eight hours—especially since Evangeline wasn't due on the set until late afternoon—but I knew I'd probably only take four and then get up and just... wait. I wasn't expecting any problems, but I'd feel better being awake and standing guard.

Not that it was appreciated.

With a weary sigh, I stood and pulled off my belt and tossed it. My hand was on my button fly when I heard a blood-curdling scream. Immediately I was running toward Evangeline's room, but unfortunately, the door was locked. Without hesitation, I kicked it down.

And that hurt like a son of a bitch.

"Evangeline!" I called out. She wasn't in her room, and nothing there looked out of place. The bathroom door wasn't locked, and I quickly stepped inside and found her in the corner on the floor wrapped in a towel. She was soaking wet, and I couldn't tell if she was crying or not. "Evangeline?

What happened?" I kept my eyes on her face to try to keep her calm.

She was pale. Too pale. And she was trembling.

"Evangeline? Sweetheart? What's going on?" I asked softly, my hands gently grasping her shoulders, looking for any signs of injury.

One hand reached out and shakily pointed to the linen closet. Slowly I stood and turned toward the closet. I stopped and looked over my shoulder at her one more time. I thought she was shaking even more. Going back to her, I lifted her in my arms and carried her out to the bedroom and gently placed her on the bed before going back into the bathroom.

"Son of a bitch," I muttered and stopped at the open door.

There, on a bed of white towels, were the heads of three decapitated rats.

SEVEN
Evangeline

I'd been living with fear for weeks now, but I'd never in my life been as terrified as this.

The stalker was in my apartment. *My apartment.* Despite all the security I had surrounding me, he was actually inside my bathroom—to put those horrible, sickening rats in my linen closet.

Phone calls and messages were bad enough. They made you feel exposed, vulnerable, at the mercy of someone else's will. But an intrusion like this was something worse, something more. This apartment wasn't my home—it was just the place I was staying while I shot this film. But it still felt like my private space, and it was a horrible violation, as well as an obvious threat.

If he could get into this place—despite Cole's best efforts—then he could get to me anywhere, anytime he wanted.

Nowhere I went would be safe.

I was huddled in a ball on my bed, still wearing nothing but a towel and wet hair, and I was trying to talk myself into pulling it together. But I couldn't. I kept seeing those mutilated bodies on the white towels. Here. Where it was supposed to be safe.

A wave of nausea slammed into me as Cole came back into the bedroom, looking as grim as anyone I'd ever seen.

He would be beating himself up. I knew exactly how he was feeling. And ironically, despite everything, I felt a pull of empathy—recognizing how badly he'd feel about this failure and how much he would take it to heart.

"Get up," he said. "We're getting out of here."

I blinked at him, uncomprehending. When he'd found me in the bathroom, he'd been protective, almost tender. He'd called me "sweetheart." A little part of me had heard the words and liked them.

But he was nothing like that now. He was cool and hard and professional, and it was like a slap in the face.

"Get up," he repeated. "We can't stay here. The apartment has been compromised. I need to get you somewhere safe."

It made sense, even through the fuzziness of my mind, but I couldn't get my body to react immediately. "The rats...," I began, hit with more intense nausea as the picture of the bloody corpses revived in my mind.

"I'll have someone collect them for evidence," he said, "but you're not staying here a minute longer. Get up. Right now."

He wasn't rude as much as coolly efficient, and it was almost a relief now. Something I could cling to, something sane and competent in a world that was nothing but sickening chaos. I tried to sit up and halfway managed it, and then Cole reached out to pull me to my feet.

I swayed and my knees buckled briefly, but he kept me upright.

I was starting to get my body under control when I saw that my top dresser drawer was partway opened.

I never left drawers opened. They always bugged me if they weren't closed all the way.

I gripped Cole's arm urgently and choked. "The drawer. He was in my…" I couldn't finish the sentence. I felt the blood drain out of my face for the second time in less than five minutes.

I kept my lingerie in my top dresser drawer. And this monster's hands would have been all over them.

All of it. Everything. Violated.

The nausea hit again, and this time it was too much. I started to gag as my body violently rejected what my mind simply couldn't accept. There was no way I could go into the master bath again, so I ran for the half bath in the hallway, making it just in time to vomit into the toilet.

I was on my knees on the floor, tears streaming down my face when I was done.

Cole was there too, lifting me to my feet, wiping my face with a damp hand towel, letting me lean on him.

"Let's get out of here," he said, one of his arms holding me against his body. I needed his warmth and his strength, so I couldn't possibly pull away yet. "You can't stay here any longer."

"Okay." My throat was raspy, and I was still shaking, but the idea of leaving this horrible place was such a relief that I managed to straighten up. "I need clothes."

Cole helped me to a chair in the hallway and then went back into the bedroom. He returned with my phone and some clothes for me to put on.

Millions had seen me mostly naked, so I wasn't particularly bothered with modesty. I was too upset to worry about it now anyway. I dropped the towel and pulled on the underwear, leggings, and oversized sweater he'd brought me, without making much effort to hide myself from Cole.

He kept his head turned away from me—out of general civility, I assumed—but he didn't turn his back, and he didn't leave the hall.

When I was dressed, we collected what he needed and my bag, and we left. Cole made sure I was safely in the chauffeured car before he started to contact people and make a plan.

I sure wouldn't want to be on the receiving end of the tone he was using with everyone he talked to. Of course, I actually had been on the receiving end of a similar tone from him, and it had only made me angry. But he was different now. Like there was a dangerous coldness to his anger that he'd never shown to me.

He made arrangements for the police to come and for the rats to be collected as evidence. "Should we wait for the police?" I asked when he hung up on one of his calls. "Won't they want to talk to us?"

"Yes, but you're not going to hang around here. You can talk to the police tomorrow."

I opened my mouth to ask another question, but he was already on a different call. I listened to a blistering interrogation about the security of the apartment building until he got out of the car to have the phone conversations right outside the car.

He didn't leave me alone even though he was no longer in the car. Someone would still have to get through him to get to me.

It made me feel a little better—even his anger did—knowing the stalker would have to face that anger if he made a move on me directly.

I was at loose ends and wanted to do something, so I dialed up Sebastian's number without thinking.

He wouldn't be able to help me—since he was far away—but he was my friend and I needed all I could get right now.

"Hey," Sebastian said, picking up on the fourth ring. "What's the matter?"

It was kind of late. He probably hadn't expected to be interrupted. So I told him about the rats without preamble.

"Shit," Sebastian breathed when I was finished. There was a pause as he obviously tried to take it in. Then, "Shit."

"It's... horrible."

"Where's Cole?"

"He's working on it. He's right outside the car."

"How the hell could he have gotten into the apartment?"

"That's what Cole is trying to figure out."

"Where are you going now?"

"I don't know. Cole said he needed to get me out of the apartment, and I couldn't possibly stay there now anyway. He said he was going to take me to somewhere safe, but I don't know where could be safe enough."

"My family has a place in DC with security like Fort Knox. It's usually used for visiting executives, but it's empty a lot of time. No one is in it this week. You can stay there if you don't mind the drive."

"I don't. I just want to be somewhere safe."

"It's safe. I promise. We've used it before for a couple of our security jobs. Cole will know where it is."

"That sounds good," I said, startled when the car door opened without warning and Cole crawled in beside me.

"What sounds good?" he demanded, frowning intensely at seeing me on the phone. "Who is that?"

"Sebastian. He has an idea about where we can go."

I'd barely gotten the sentence out when Cole was taking the phone from my hands and talking to Sebastian himself. He didn't sound very friendly. He didn't sound anything like friends.

I wondered if he was annoyed with Sebastian for some reason or if he was always this way. He definitely wasn't the warm-fuzzy type.

Cole evidently agreed with staying in the Maxwell place, and he handed me the phone back when he was done.

"Why did you call Sebastian?" he demanded in clipped tones.

I blinked, distracted from the fear that was starting to make me shiver again. "What do you mean?"

"I assume you called him and he didn't call you."

"No, he didn't call me. I called him. Why shouldn't I? This whole thing is appalling."

"I know it's appalling. What I don't know is what he could do about it."

"What's the matter with you?" I snapped, the surge of annoyance almost a relief since it was familiar and controllable. "He's your partner, and he had a good idea about where we could stay. He's also a friend of mine."

"I know he is."

I peered at his face, realizing he was offended or hurt or something about my asking Sebastian for help, rather than relying completely on him. From the time we'd spent together already, I knew how independent and self-sufficient and unbreakably proud he was. Maybe he saw the innocuous call as a slight on his abilities.

It wasn't, of course. Despite what I'd said to Cole over the past week, I didn't think anyone could have done a better job than he'd done. There were forces at work here that were beyond the scope of one man to get a handle on, but if anyone could do it, Cole could.

I didn't call Sebastian because I didn't trust Cole to keep me safe, but maybe Cole thought I had.

"Have you always been this way?" I asked, genuinely wanting the answer, even though the reflections had all been in my mind, so the question was out of the blue.

"What way?" Cole's eyes searched my face.

"Like you have to conquer the world single-handedly."

He looked briefly surprised but not offended as I'd half expected. "That's pretty much the way it's always worked."

"Maybe because you refuse to accept help when it's offered."

"Help usually comes with strings."

His expression was slightly closed off, but I could tell he meant it. His experiences had taught him not to rely on anyone but himself.

"Even from friends?" I asked softly. He wasn't completely alone. He had real friends. Close friends. Surely that would make a difference.

Something broke on his face very briefly, and his lips parted like he might speak. But he didn't. He gave his head a little shake and turned away from me.

~

We didn't talk much on the drive to DC, and unfortunately, that left me too much time to brood over what had just happened.

Every way I looked at it, it was a nightmare. The stalker had access to my apartment, which meant he was incredibly talented at breaking and entering or he was using someone I trusted.

Or maybe he *was* someone I trusted.

I couldn't stand the idea of it, and by the time we'd gotten to the gated street and the expensive townhouse owned by the prestigious Maxwell family, I was almost sick again at the thought of such a betrayal.

The townhouse was as safe as we could want it to be—complete with neighborhood security, top-of-the-line alarms, limited access to the outside, and even a panic room.

If I was going to feel safe anywhere, it would be here.

I was still trembling as Cole showed me to a bedroom. It was obviously the master since the panic room was attached. It was decorated with big antiques and lush colors, but I hardly noticed the décor.

"Are you okay?" Cole asked. He'd been watching me a lot, but I had no idea what he was thinking.

"Yes." I wasn't sure I was okay, but what else could I say? I put my bag down on the bed and felt strangely tiny next to the high mattress and huge walnut posters. And then something hit me. Turning, I said, "I want my life back. I can't stand this constant out of control feeling." I began to pace. "I'm so tired of being scared and right now—more than anything else—I'm angry."

He studied me for a long moment before walking over and taking me by the hand.

"What are you...?"

"I know exactly what will help," he said cryptically as he led me through the main floor and then down a flight of stairs. He hit a switch on the wall and released my hand. "What do you think?"

Looking around, I was mildly unimpressed. "It's a gym," I said. "I don't think a couple of miles on the treadmill is going to help with this rage I'm feeling."

He laughed softly. "No, I wouldn't imagine so. But what about the opportunity to punch something?"

Not that got my attention.

He nodded toward the far corner of the room, and sure enough, there was a large punching bag hanging from the ceiling. Never in my life had I considered punching anything, but right now, I could see the appeal.

Cole must have read the interest on my face because he grinned and motioned for me to follow him. He turned on more lights and grabbed a couple of pairs of boxing gloves.

"I have to admit, I was going to come down here and do this after you went to sleep," he admitted. "But after what you just admitted, I figured you could probably benefit from a little time with the bag too."

"I've never hit anything in my life," I said with a small laugh. "I never wanted to."

He looked at me with one dark brow arched. "Really? Even me?"

I couldn't even try and suppress my laugh. "Okay, I'll admit, I've been very tempted to punch you a time or two."

"Well, now's your chance."

My eyes went wide. "What? I thought you said I was going to punch the bag?"

He smiled. A real smile. I couldn't help but soften at the sight. This was the first time I ever saw him so relaxed—which was crazy considering the night we'd had so far.

He didn't respond right away. First he helped me get the gloves on, and he tied them tight to secure them. Then he took care of his own.

I couldn't believe how incredibly sexy he looked.

"Okay, I'm going to walk you through some of the basic moves so you don't overextend and hurt yourself," he explained. "We'll take it slow, and then you'll practice hitting my hands and then the bag. Sound good?"

I nodded, anxious to start.

For the next several minutes, Cole explained how to stand and how to move my arms in a way that was controlled for maximum impact. At first it felt a little bit awkward, but I found my rhythm, and soon I was mirroring his moves. It was almost like a choreographed dance.

He stopped and came to stand in front of me—his hands held out in front of him. "Okay, I want you to use your right hand to punch my left," he explained. "Ready?"

I nodded again and then followed his direction. Pulling back, I then put all my energy into making contact with his glove. When it did, it was the best feeling. I looked at Cole and smiled. "How was that?"

He chuckled. "Not bad, slugger. Now let's try using your left hand to punch my right."

After alternating several times, he showed me how to work the bag. I stood back mesmerized as I watched him move. His T-shirt was snug and didn't hide the play of muscles on his back, his arms. I always knew Cole was strong and muscular, but to see him in action like this was almost hypnotic.

"You ready to try?" he asked, totally taking me by surprise.

"Uh…"

"You can pretend it's my face you're punching."

At that moment, punching him was the last thing on my mind.

Cole stepped around me and then pressed up close against my back. "C'mon, Maybelline," he murmured, "you know you want to hit me."

I knew what he was doing—taunting me so I'd step up to the bag and start swinging. I already felt a little bit better after the few punches I'd done against his hands, how much better would I feel after letting loose on the bag?

"What's the matter, princess," he added smoothly, "too prissy to work up a sweat?"

And that was all it took. I stepped in close and punched the bag once. Then again.

And then I couldn't seem to stop.

I punched for every scary phone call, for all the twisted deliveries, for all the times my life had been turned upside down by a sick individual, and then I punched some more for all the times Cole had teased me.

I was panting and breathing heavy and let out a kind of a primal scream when Cole stepped up behind me and urged me to step back and take a break.

"Easy there, Tiger," he said. "I don't want you to hurt yourself."

I knew enough about working out to know that you didn't want to overdo it on a new exercise, but this just felt so good. Which is what I told him.

He nodded and laughed again. "I know. But this is going to be home for at least a little while so you can come down here any time and work out all of your anger and frustration."

It was little consolation at the moment, but I knew I needed to be careful. No need to add muscle aches to the growing list of things messing with my life.

"Five more minutes," he said as he took a step away. "I'm going to go and grab us some water. I'll be right back."

I immediately took advantage of the time and pounded on the bag a bit more. By the time Cole was back with two bottles of water, I was ready to call it a day.

He helped me remove my gloves and then handed me my drink. We stood in companionable silence while we cooled down. Soon we were turning off the lights and heading back up the stairs.

"Do you want anything to eat?" he asked as we walked by the kitchen. "There isn't much here, but we could probably whip up something."

"No. It's late." I swallowed and toed off my shoes. "I think I'll just shower and go to bed."

"That sounds like a good plan."

I walked away and took a quick shower. It felt good after working out. When I stepped out of the bathroom a few minutes later wearing nothing but my panties an oversized t-shirt, I was surprised to find Cole standing in the bedroom.

He nodded toward the chaise under the large window. "I'm going to sleep there. I'm not going to leave you alone. Not even to sleep."

I wasn't annoyed by this high-handedness. It was a relief. I didn't want to be alone. It terrified me. "Okay."

Cole went into the bathroom while I was crawling under the covers, and he returned wearing his pants but no shirt and no shoes.

He might look like he was ready for bed, but I didn't really think he was going to sleep.

I was damned sure I wasn't going to sleep tonight.

I'd fallen into a strange, blank daze by going through the motions of everyday routines, but the fear hit me again when Cole turned off the overhead light, leaving the big room lit by only the bedside light

"You'll be safe here," he said, his eyes searching my face again, as if looking for signs of an impending collapse.

I wasn't entirely confident the collapse was at bay. It could hit me at any minute.

"If you keep acting all nice with me, I'll know for sure the situation is desperate." I managed a ghost of a smile.

He gave a soft huff of amusement. "You call this nice?"

"Well, relatively speaking since you're usually all mean and snappish."

"I'm pretty sure I've snapped my fair share this evening." He'd stepped over close to me, and I reached to hold on to his arm, needing stability, needing *something*.

"Yeah. But it feels like it's in a nicer way."

He smiled faintly, that intensity still holding his gaze with mine, like neither of us could look away. "That's me. Snappishly nice."

I couldn't hold back a little giggle, but even as I was laughing, the vision of those decapitated rats hit me again, and the giggle transformed into a gurgle that turned into a choked sob. The boxing had been a great distraction, but now that all was quiet, everything came rushing back.

Embarrassed by the sudden breakdown, I turned away from Cole so he wouldn't see my changed expression.

"Shit," he muttered, turning me back around and pulling me against him. "You're safe here, Evangeline. I promise."

I clung to him, feeling small and weak and too scared. "I don't feel safe."

His arms tightened around me. "What can I do to make you feel safer?"

"Stay with me," I whispered, stroking his hard back and feeling the strength of him in the lines and muscles. "Stay with me tonight."

"I already told you I would." His voice was slightly hoarse, and his body was feeling tense.

It was a tension that spoke to me though—that I wanted to feel even more, that seemed to hold the nightmare at bay.

"No." I pulled back enough to look up at his face and deep eyes. "I want you stay with me. All the way."

He couldn't fail to know what I was talking about. It was obvious in the way I was touching him, in the way I was gazing up at him. And I knew he wanted it too. That tension was arousal as much as anything else.

For a moment a flicker of conflict was visible on his face, but then it disappeared in a wave of passion. He reached down to take my face in both his hands the way he had before, and he released a soft groan as he leaned down into a kiss.

The kiss was just as hungry as the first one had been, but it felt even needier, more desperate this time. He seemed to need me as much as I needed him.

Our lips and tongues tangled as I pressed my body against his, wanting to feel how big and hard and capable he was by the feel of his body.

I was already turned on, despite the trauma of earlier in the evening, but my need was as much emotional as physical—as if Cole and his strength was the only thing holding off the darkness.

His hands slid down to cup my bottom, and he pressed me against his groin, which had hardened in an obvious way.

He broke the kiss briefly to mutter, "Sometimes trauma can lead to this sort of thing. It might just be the trauma that's making you think you want this."

I groaned in frustration because I wanted to kiss him again. My hands were sliding over the firm skin of his bare back, and my fingers squeezed under his waistband to reach even lower. "Why does it matter why I want this? I want this. So much. Right now." I rubbed myself against his arousal until he groaned. "Don't you?"

"You know damned well I do."

"So take what you want."

He groaned again, differently this time, and kissed me again. This time the kiss took us into the bed, and I wrapped my legs around him as he buried his face against my neck, nibbling and kissing in a way that made me squirm.

When I was fumbling with the button on his pants, he wrapped his fingers around my wrist to stop me. "Slow down, sweetheart," he murmured thickly. He moved my arm so it was lying on the bed beside me. "Slow down."

I was panting and flushed, wanting to bury myself in the sensations so I could forget about everything else. I moaned in frustration and arched up into his body. "I don't want to slow down."

He gave me a wolfish smile. "But it will be better that way."

Despite his words, his expression and his touch were neither teasing nor playful. They were intense, unexpectedly gentle as he pulled the T-shirt off over my head and started to kiss and caress his way down my body.

I could see how much he liked my body by the way his eyes heated up. It was thrilling, intoxicating, that this strong, capable man wanted me so much.

His mouth closed over one of my nipples, and the soft touch was almost torturous. I couldn't keep my hips still as I clawed lines down his back in my frustration.

"Cole, please," I gasped, fisting one of my hands in his hair.

He lifted his head. "Let me give this to you, sweetheart."

My mouth parted with a silent cry when his hand slipped between my legs and found my wet arousal. Then the cry found its voice when he started to pump with two fingers.

I rode his fingers eagerly as an orgasm built up and then broke inside me. I was panting loudly when I came down from the high, and my body relaxed a little.

But then Cole was being gentle again, kissing his way softly down my belly.

"Cole, please," I said again in a slightly different tone this time.

He looked up again at my words. "I want to give you more. Especially after everything that's happened. I didn't want to be rough. I want it to be…"

He didn't finish, but I understood what he meant. And it touched me. He was trying to be careful, to be gentle, to make sure this was good for me—no matter what his own body demanded.

But he didn't understand what I wanted at all.

I shook my head and reached up to cup his rugged face. "But I don't want soft and gentle. I want… I need for you to be… strong." I saw his expression change, so I repeated, "I want to feel you be strong. Please, Cole. Be strong for me."

"Damn right, I will," he said gruffly, the tension in his body transforming palpably. The fire blazed up in his eyes even more, and I knew that, at last, he was going to give us what we both wanted from tonight.

EIGHT
Cole

It was wrong.

So damn wrong.

But for some reason, it made complete sense.

I was a selfish bastard—particularly in the bedroom. Normally, women worked for it a little. I wasn't necessarily proud of that fact, but it was normally what I liked. But right now with Evangeline? I wanted to be the one working—the one giving.

And I wanted to give it hard.

I wasn't sure she knew what she was asking for.

I looked down at her again; her eyes were glazed with passion. Her lips were parted. And she was the sexiest thing I'd ever seen. All I wanted was to pound into her. To fuck her until she couldn't remember her own name—let alone what had happened earlier.

I stood and quickly undressed before reclaiming my spot on the bed on top of her. The feel of her naked flesh beneath mine was both heaven and hell.

Taking her hands, I placed them above her head on the pillow. Her eyes went a little wide, and it made me smile. "Brace yourself, princess." She stiffened slightly, and that made me pause. "We don't have to do anything you don't want to. You know that, right?"

She nodded. "I know what I want, Cole. It's just... no one's ever... been like this with me. I don't want to disappoint you."

If I'd been standing, she would have brought me to my knees. "That's not even possible," I told her, and I meant it. Just the mere fact that she was here, that she wanted me, and she trusted me was one of the greatest moments of my life.

She squirmed beneath me, and I knew I had to do something now. "Sweetheart, I promise we'll stop if I do anything you don't like."

"Cole?"

"Hmm?"

"Stop talking."

A slow smile spread across my face before I could even stop it. I loved a woman who told me what she wanted. Rather than answer her, I gave her exactly what she wanted.

Holding her hands still, I kissed her. Hard. Her tongue mated with mine, and I heard a small whimper escape, but I didn't stop.

My mouth left hers and nipped at her jaw, her throat, her collarbone—all the way to her breasts. I'd been fantasizing about those more than any man should. I teased first one nipple and then the other, making her cry out. I bit at the tender flesh until she cried out again and arched beneath me.

But I didn't stop.

Releasing her hands, I let mine begin to follow the path my mouth had just been on. Gently my rough skin slid along hers, and I marveled at her softness. I don't think I'd ever felt a woman with silkier skin. I could touch her for days and still not get enough.

I teased at her belly button until my hands were anchored at her waist. "Spread your legs for me, sweetheart," I murmured thickly. She hesitated, and I lifted my head and met her nervous gaze. It couldn't be possible that no one had ever...

"Cole."

"I bet you taste sweet, Evangeline. Let me taste you. Please."

Slowly her legs opened farther, and I could see the slight tremble in her thighs. My hands soothed them as I lowered my lips to taste her.

Heaven.

I heard her low, throaty sigh, and it was almost enough to make me come. I kind of felt like I was corrupting her.

"More, Cole. More," she panted.

Never say that I don't aim to please. I feasted on her until she was sobbing my name, and when I thought she couldn't take anymore, I felt her come apart, my name on her lips the entire time. I soothed her. I gently stroked her thighs, her belly, her breasts as I made my way back up to her mouth and quieted her sobs with my own lips.

She wrapped around me—all long, silky limbs—and I knew I was on the brink. I broke the kiss and reached for where I'd dropped my pants and fumbled for a condom. I slipped it on in record time, a sheen of sweat forming on my body from trying to hold back.

Then I braced myself over her, holding her hands. I was going to ask if she was ready, but I already knew the answer. I surged forward and watched her eyes grow wide again—something I was really beginning to love—and buried myself to the hilt.

"You're so... you're..."

I knew what she was going to say, and at that moment, I didn't want to talk. I didn't want her to talk. I wanted to feel. For both of us to just feel. I ducked my head and claimed her mouth with mine again. I didn't wait, my tongue thrust forward to dual with hers just as I began to move inside her.

There was no slow buildup.

There was no time to get acquainted.

I didn't do emotional with sex. I liked to fuck. And on any given day, with any given woman, I liked to fuck hard. That was what my body was doing, and Evangeline was going wild beneath me—meeting me thrust for thrust and loving it. But my head? My heart? Well, something was going on there, and I couldn't stop to examine it too closely.

So I let my body do what it does best.

She was so tight around me. So wet. So... everything.

"Come for me, baby," I whispered against her ear. "Do it for me again."

"I can't," she murmured, her head thrashing back and forth. I pounded into her harder and harder, my grip on her hands near brutal.

"Come on, sweetheart. Do it for me." I shifted just slightly and hit the spot that sent her soaring. Evangeline screamed my name as she wrapped herself so tight around me there was no way to tell where one body ended and the other began.

I did my best to hold back, to let her have her moment, but I couldn't. The feel of her, the sound of her, the smell of her—I was on sensory overload. This time it was me crying out her name as I came. I couldn't stop myself. Sex was never personal for me before, but this time it was.

It so fucking was.

~

It was about four in the morning, and I was staring at the ceiling. I hadn't slept at all. Beside me, Evangeline was curled against me with her hand on my chest and one leg thrown over mine. We'd made love several more times over the course of the night—each more explosive than the next.

Turned out she likes it a little rough.

I couldn't help but smile. The woman was constantly surprising me.

I should have been sleeping. I needed the rest—especially after everything we'd just done, but I couldn't. I was in foreign territory, and my mind was spinning out of control. I didn't *do* the all-night thing. Not the sex. That was never been a problem. But staying until morning? Uh… yeah. That was the issue.

As good as Evangeline felt in my arms, I kept thinking I should *want* to leave. It was weird. I wasn't… I wasn't mentally prepared for this. Last night was amazing. It was every fantasy come true, but we were both keyed up—in a charged situation. This wasn't real. It couldn't be.

When she woke up, I was going to need to make sure she understood that. This didn't make us a couple, and there was certainly no future in it. It was a onetime thing.

Okay, technically, it was a three-time thing, but that was it. No more. I'd just rest my eyes for a minute, and then I was going to get up, put on my pants, and go sleep on the lounge like I had originally planned.

It was what I had to do.

The next time I opened my eyes, the sun was up and Evangeline was on top of me, kissing my chest. Her movements were slow and languid, and she was so warm that I had to hold her close with one hand while the other anchored itself in her glorious mane of hair.

She whispered my name as she moved her way down my body, much like I had done to hers last night. And when I felt her breath teasing at my hardened length, I was lost.

Okay, so it was going to be a four-time thing. And I was completely okay with it.

~

I did eventually get up from the bed. It wasn't easy, but I managed it.

Evangeline had fallen back to sleep after our latest romp, and I knew I needed to get up and call the guys and let them know what was going on. Things were getting a bit out of control, and as much as I hated to admit it, I was stumped as to what was going on with this case. I was no closer to finding the stalker, and now that I'd slept with Evangeline, I wasn't sure how objective I could be.

I was not sharing that last bit of information with the guys. For starters, I'd been giving them all shit since we started doing this about their love lives. I knew they were all just itching for the chance to return the favor. The only difference between them and me was the fact that they were in love with the women they got involved with. I was not in love with Evangeline, but I was sure they'd try to tell me otherwise.

My lips were sealed.

I dialed Levi first because he was the one who gets the whole conference-call thing going all the time. I would give him the basics and wait while he got the guys on the line.

"Cole, hey," Levi said a little sleepily as he answered the phone. "What's up?"

I told him about the break-in at Evangeline's apartment. "We're at Sebastian's family's place now. I just thought you guys should know and wanted to get some insight. I'm losing my damn mind on this case, trying to figure out what the hell's going on, but the list of potential suspects never seems to shrink."

"That's because she's a public figure. The threat could be coming from anywhere in the world. It might not be someone who is acting alone. It could be..." He stopped. "You know what? Let me get Seb and Declan on the line, and we'll talk about it. Hang on a sec while I get them."

"Great. Thanks, Levi." Levi was one of the good guys. He was the most levelheaded one of the group. He was a good leader and a good friend. He knew when to call bullshit and when to play cheerleader. I already felt better after our brief conversation.

Two minutes later, the four of us were on the line. "How is Evangeline?" Sebastian asked, concern lacing his tone.

"She's shook up. She doesn't feel safe anywhere, and I can't blame her. I can't figure out how anyone got in, but last night I didn't take the time to do the questioning. It was a crapshoot, and my main concern was to get her out of there. I know you guys might not agree but—"

"No, no," Sebastian said, "you did the right thing. I had some of our guys go over there with the local police last night and look everything over, check for prints and all that stuff. I haven't heard back from anyone yet. But I planned on following up this morning."

"Thanks. I appreciate it." I did. But at the same time, I hated that someone had to come in and clean up after me. They'd all had their share of cases, and in all of them, they tended to be able to wrap them up themselves.

"Okay, so let's wait until we get a report back this morning before we jump to any conclusions. The important thing is to keep Evangeline safe. Is everything all right there, Cole?" Declan asked.

"Yeah. This place is guarded as well as Fort Knox. We got in last night, and I know no one followed us. I've got all the blinds closed and curtains drawn. It's like a cave in here, but I don't want anyone seeing in."

"That's good. You just focus on keeping her calm," Levi said. "Sebastian, I want you to follow up with our guys and see what they found at Evangeline's apartment. I'm going to get in touch with Evangeline's security people and let them know that something's happened, but I'm not going to tell them what. As far as I'm concerned, they're still suspects too. Declan, I'd like you to try to get a lead on any film footage of the movie set and from the area around where Cole and Evangeline have been staying. Anything. Parking lot cameras, fan video, anything. We'll have our guys analyze it and see who's showing up when they shouldn't be."

"What about me?" I asked.

"Just keep Evangeline safe and inside," Sebastian said. "That's the most important thing right now.

"Great. So you're all doing my job, and I have to sit here and play babysitter? I'm not useless, you know! I realize this shit went down on my watch, but that doesn't mean I have to be treated like an idiot."

"No one's treating you like an idiot, Cole," Levi said diplomatically. "You've built a relationship with Evangeline. She trusts you. She needs a bodyguard, and you're right there. It only makes sense for you to stay close to her."

"What? I'm not close to her! What the hell are you talking about?"

"Oh no," Sebastian muttered and then cursed. "Please tell me you haven't done anything stupid. Tell me you didn't sleep with her."

"Fuck you, Sebastian," I said. "Unlike the rest of you, I don't fuck around on the job. I'm here because you forced me to be here. I can't wait for this case to be over so I can get the hell out of here!"

"Okay, okay." Levi interrupted. "Everyone go back to their corners. It's too early in the morning for fighting." He sighed. "Is everyone clear on what they need to do?"

We all murmured our agreement.

"Well, while I have you all on the phone, I have some other news."

"Please tell me you're not having another baby already," Declan teased.

Levi chuckled. "Definitely not. It's hard to believe that such a small person is so loud and demanding. He's running the show around here, and Harper and I are dying for a full-night's sleep."

"You'll get there eventually," Sebastian said. "And you'll forget all about these nights."

"I don't know about that." He paused. "The report on Gavin is going to be released in two weeks. I got the call asking if we wanted to be there in DC when it's read."

"What did you tell them?" Declan asked.

"I told them I'd talk to all of you. And now I am."

"Are you going?" he asked again.

"I am," Levi said. "I think I need to."

"Me too," Sebastian said, and Declan immediately agreed.

That left me. Dammit.

"As long as this case is over, I'll be there too," I said reluctantly.

"If it's not, we'll send a team over to keep an eye on Evangeline for the day so you can come with us. I think we owe it to Gavin to all be there together."

I knew it was the right thing to do, but I still didn't want to do it. Unfortunately, I didn't see a way out.

"Yeah, okay."

"All right. So we're all on the same page," Levi confirmed and then got back to business. "Seb, call as soon as you hear anything."

"I will," he replied and then paused. "Cole?"

"Yeah?"

"I'm serious, man, do *not* sleep with her."

"What's the matter? I'm not good enough for your friend?"

Sebastian huffed with annoyance. "Seriously? What is it with you?"

"Why the warning then?"

"Look, all I'm saying is that this is a... special case. She's a celebrity. She's in the spotlight, and right now she's completely freaked out and vulnerable. Just don't do anything stupid."

"Whatever. Don't worry. My low-life hands won't touch your pristine little friend." *Again.* "So save your worrying for someone else."

"Cole," he said with exasperation.

"What?" I snapped.

"Look, I'm going to make the calls, and then I'm going to come there—to the house."

"Why?" Suspicion made me tense up.

"I'll bring food and whatever other essentials you may need, and I just want to check on Evangeline."

Yeah, right. It was more like he was coming here to check on me and make sure I wasn't dirtying up his precious little friend.

"I gotta go. Call when you have something useful to say." And then I hung up and tossed the phone on the couch. I turned around to pace and ran right into Evangeline.

She was tousled-looking, and I actually felt myself starting to sweat because she was sleepy and sexy, and I had an overwhelming need to take her back to bed and make love to her again. Only this time it would be slow and sweet.

I was totally screwed.

I could hear Sebastian's voice in my head—the tone, the condemnation—and knew what I had to do.

"All the blinds are closed, and they need to stay that way. Curtains too. Sebastian's going to come by today. He's going to bring food and supplies and whatnot. Until he gets here, just stay out of sight. Understand?" My tone was firm, businesslike, and I could see instantly that she was hurt by it.

It was the right thing for me to do.

No matter how much it sucked.

She walked farther into the room and stopped a few feet away from me. "What's going on? Did... did I do something wrong?" The vulnerability in her voice, the slight tremor, coupled with the way she looked almost did me in.

"It's another day," I said, softening my tone a bit. "I... I have to focus on finding the person who's stalking you. I can't... I can't do this with you."

"But last night—"

"Was last night," I said, effectively cutting her off. "It can't be more than that. I need to do my job so you can get back to yours."

She took a step back. "Oh. Okay."

But I knew it wasn't. I knew she wasn't used to this sort of thing. The guys in her life probably catered to her and were all about the morning after and talks of the future. Better she should realize now that it was not like that with us—and it was never going to be like that.

And damn if that didn't disappoint me.

"You need to go and shower and get cleaned up. If Sebastian sees you like that, he'll freak out."

Right before my eyes, she transformed. Gone was the vulnerability from a moment ago, and in its place was a hint of a tigress.

"And you don't want him seeing that you touched his pristine little friend with your low-life hands?" She arched a brow and crossed her arms over her chest as she threw my words to Sebastian back at me.

I smirked. "Yeah. Something like that."

I guess she liked how I didn't try to lie or make an excuse for what I'd said. She relaxed her stance a bit and took a step toward me again. "Cole, listen. I—"

"Really, Evangeline, you need to go and get ready. I have no idea how soon before Sebastian arrives."

"But I just wanted to—"

"I have calls to make." I interrupted and reached over and picked up my phone and strode from the room. I didn't know what she wanted to say, and if I stayed that close to her any longer, it wouldn't matter what she wanted to say because I would have taken her again—right there on the living room floor.

No matter how pristine she was.

And no matter how wrong it really was.

NINE
Evangeline

Cole was making a last-ditch effort to be professional.

I could understand. This was his job, and he must pride himself on being good at it. Sleeping with a client was hardly the way to get a gold star in the bodyguard hall of fame. So when he backed off this morning and acted all cool and aloof, I knew exactly where it was coming from.

At first his quick turnaround might have hurt my feelings a bit, but then I'd thought it through. Now it was annoying but understandable.

It didn't discourage me at all. Sex with Cole was the best sex I'd ever had in my life, and it would be unforgivably stupid to assume it was just a onetime (or four times) thing. I wasn't dreaming this was love eternal or anything silly like that, but what Cole and I had going was just too good to let go.

He could pretend to be professional all he wanted. I definitely didn't want him distracted from catching this stalker, after all. But as soon as it wasn't a crisis situation anymore, I was definitely going to get him in bed again.

I knew he wanted me too, so it wouldn't be too hard to maneuver.

I was feeling better than I had before about life in general when Sebastian came over a half hour later. I was finishing getting dressed when he arrived, and when I came out, he and Cole were talking over coffee.

The look Cole shot me was very hands-off, so I went over to hug Sebastian and then just gave Cole a cool look. "So what's the plan?" I asked, looking from man to man.

They were both strong, intelligent, and exceptionally competent. If a woman was going to be safe from a stalker, I was.

"That's under discussion," Sebastian said, smiling at me. "Cole thinks you should stay here."

I glanced over at Cole, who was giving me a mild form of his glower. "I wouldn't be opposed to that. What are you guys going to do?"

"Seb can stay here with you, and I can get out there and catch this asshole."

I tried not to roll my eyes. Naturally, now he wanted to get as far away from me as possible. "Do you have a plan for catching the asshole?"

"I've got some ideas."

I looked back to Sebastian. "Are they good ideas?"

Cole bristled visibly at the implications of my question, but I ignored him. I could act just as standoffish as he could, after all.

Sebastian gave a half shrug. "Eh. All we can do at this point is stab around in the dark."

"We need to draw the stalker out then," I said, realizing what the problem was, why both men were acting wary. "If I'm cooped up in this safe house, then all you can do is wait and hope you land on something. I need to get back out on set, don't I?"

Cole and Sebastian looked at each other before they both looked at me.

"Your safety is our primary concern," Sebastian said. "You'll be safer if you stay here."

"Maybe, but you don't have any leads on his identity yet, do you?" I looked from one to the other and saw the answer on their faces. "So I might be safe here, but this thing will never end."

"It will end. We'll catch him one way or the other." That was Cole, and he was still bristling, but it looked like it was with defensiveness now, a muscle rippling with tension in his jaw.

"But you'll be more likely to catch him if I'm out there so he can make another move."

"We're not going to put you in danger."

"I assume you'll keep me safe, wherever I am."

"Absolutely." Cole's eyes met mine, and it felt like we were alone in the room, alone in the world.

"So I'll get back on set so we can get this thing over with." I nodded, anxious about the idea of being vulnerable again—at the memory of those dead rats in my bathroom—but I wasn't going to be a coward, and I really wanted to get this over with.

Now more than ever.

"It's her decision," Sebastian put in, when it looked like Cole might argue.

"That's right," I said. "I'm the client. I make the decisions here. I'm due back on set this afternoon, so that's what I'll do. I can stay here at night if it's okay though. I don't really want to go back to the apartment."

"That sounds like a good idea," Sebastian said, and even Cole finally nodded.

"Okay," I said, standing up. "I need to go prepare for a couple of scenes. You all figure out a plan to take care of this guy, and make sure it's a good one."

~

I was primed for danger at every turn that afternoon, so it was a little anticlimactic when nothing happened.

The scenes we were filming were actually really hard—they demanded a gritty, bleak kind of emotion I wasn't at all used to conveying—so I had to focus completely on the work. In every downtime, I would suddenly remember that the stalker might be around, and I'd search the set for signs of trouble. Cole and Sebastian were both always around, and honestly I'd be intimidated if I was a stalker trying to sneak around those two.

Maybe they scared the guy off. Or maybe he wasn't planning anything for today. One way or the other, the afternoon ended, and I was getting changed after the last shot of the day, and there was no sign of anything gruesome or scary.

I tensed up when there was a knock on the door, but it was just Janelle, delivering some scene notes from the director.

"Thanks," I said, smiling in relief that it was just the harmless assistant in her jeans and sweatshirt.

"You did really good today," she said, her blue eyes wide and sincere. "It was really great. I was almost in tears, watching."

That kind of compliment was always going to feel good. I smiled again, more sincerely this time. "Thanks. It's a really challenging role, but I'm glad I decided to do it."

"Me too. It will be great for the world to see how much range you really have."

"Yeah." I was used to everyone assuming I could only sing, dance, and look sexy, so it was nice to have someone recognize that I might actually have a little real talent hiding away somewhere. "Hopefully, it will turn out well."

"It reminded me of that episode in Paris—from the second season. Remember? When your friend almost died?"

I blinked, thinking back through the years to the cable show I'd been on and the special, serious episode that was supposed to be a tearjerker. "Good memory," I said. "It did kind of feel like that." Only not so fake and over the top.

"Matt couldn't keep his eyes off you."

It took me a minute to remember that Matt was another assistant of Pete's. He was a rather geeky young man who never said much.

Maybe it wasn't unusual for a guy to be attracted to me, but for some reason the idea of Matt standing around mooning about me was a little creepy.

Maybe he was the stalker. I'd mention it to Cole.

"Any progress with finding..." Janelle trailed off, evidently hesitating about bringing the subject up with me.

Maybe it was a little presumptuous, but I didn't care. "Not yet. But I've got a good team on the job."

"Yeah. I guess so. You know, it might be nothing, but Malcolm has been acting kind of strange this week. Skulking around and stuff."

I felt a little sliver of fear—not really fear for my safety but fear that someone I trusted as much as Malcolm could have been acting against me all this time. It was a horrifying thought.

I'd always liked Malcolm. I really didn't want it to be him.

I didn't want it to be anyone I knew and trusted. It was much easier to think it was someone like Matt.

But it had to be someone with connections to people I knew, or they never could have gotten access to all the places they had. But maybe Matt could access all the places himself. It was possible.

"I'm sure it was nothing," I said with another smile when I realized Janelle was waiting for an answer. "Malcolm was supposed to be checking things out here, so I'm sure that's what he was doing. Thanks for these." I gestured with the script notes she'd handed me earlier.

"Sure thing." She waved and smiled, walking out of the room, and I was left thinking about all the people I trusted, about which of them I might have been wrong about.

~

Cole and I drove back to the Maxwell house after we left the set. It was a long drive, but it was worth it to me to feel safe, which I wouldn't have felt at a hotel or at the apartment.

He was quiet. Much quieter than usual. I tried to make some casual conversation, but it was like trying to talk to a stone.

Finally I shook my head and stared at him. "Since when is talking off the table."

"What?" He looked at me for real for the first time, obviously surprised by my words. "What do you mean?"

"I mean, I know sex is off the table for now, but since when is talking off the table too? Or do you think that talking to me is so irresistible that you'll immediately be seduced out of your pants?"

I was rewarded for this sally by a moment of conflicted emotion on his face—half annoyance and half amusement. Amusement evidently won because he relaxed slightly. "I think my pants are safe for now."

"That's what you think. I'm good at seducing men out of their pants."

"I bet you are. But that's not going to happen again."

The words weren't flirtatious. In fact, they were slightly grumpy. But they felt familiar. Like they were really him—which I hadn't been feeling from him all day.

Because he felt more like himself, I took the risk of asking, "So what were you brooding about just now?"

He gave a little twitch of surprise. "What are you talking about?"

"I know when a guy is brooding, and you were definitely at it just now. I was wondering why. What were you thinking about?"

He just gave a half shrug, obviously not inclined to open up.

I wasn't discouraged. In fact, I kind of liked the challenge. "Surely you weren't brooding about how hung up on me you are, beating yourself up for giving in to your raging desire only to suffer now as you try to hold yourself back."

He blinked. Then made a choked sound.

I really couldn't tell if he was laughing or if I'd somehow managed to hit home. I really liked the idea of him wanting me that much, but there wasn't much sign of it at the moment.

"But seriously," I continued, "what were you thinking about?"

He sighed and leaned back in his seat slightly, staring out his window. "Gavin."

I knew who Gavin was—his friend who had died in action. "Oh. I'm sorry."

"Yeah. Thanks."

"Did something happen to bring him up?"

"Just that they've finally finished the report on the accident, and we're supposed to go hear the findings if we want."

"Oh. Well, that's good, right? It will help to have some sort of closure, won't it?"

"I guess."

I was worried by the tension on his face, and I lifted a hand to stroke his cheek. "Why wouldn't it help?"

He leaned for just a moment into my hand before he pulled away. "It depends on what they say."

"You think they're going to say something you don't want to hear?"

"I know they will."

"Maybe it won't be so bad. It wasn't your fault, after all."

"Wasn't it?"

My heart was racing, and I wanted to shake the shuddering of guilt out of him since I somehow knew it was irrational. "You said it was an accident. Those things happen. They're terrible, but they happen. You can't beat yourself up about it."

But he could. I could see he was already beating himself up, and if he heard anything that implied he could have done something different, something to keep the accident from happening, then he would continue to beat himself up for the rest of his life.

Maybe it was better to not know than to know for sure you could have done better.

I had no idea what to say, but I wanted to make him feel better, so I scooted over in the back seat and wrapped my arms around him in a soft hug. "I don't think it was your fault, Cole."

He didn't pull out of my embrace. In fact, he wrapped one arm around me to pull me closer. "What do you know?" he muttered. The words sounded rather rude, but I could feel that he was taking comfort from me, so I wasn't offended.

"I know just as much as you. Go to the meeting and hear what they say. Running away from it isn't going to do any good."

He made a grunt of a sound and tightened his arm.

I didn't know if he was feeling better or if he was annoyed by my prying or what. But I felt confident, like I'd done the right thing.

And I sure wasn't going to complain about being this close to him.

After a minute, I couldn't resist anymore, so I stroked my hand up his hard chest, over his shirt. His body was firm and warm and rough, and it felt delicious against my hand.

When I reached his jaw, I stroked the skin there, feeling the slight stubble against my palm.

He was gazing down at me like he could swallow me whole, and it made my entire body come alive.

I stretched up as he leaned down, and then we were kissing hungrily, needily, our tongues dueling with passionate urgency.

I was really getting into it—my body as well as my heart—when he pulled away abruptly. "We can't do this," he said gruffly. He was sweating slightly and looked visibly strained.

Also visibly aroused.

Panting and overly warm, I tried not to whimper in disappointment. When I caught my breath, I told myself not to argue or make a fuss. He was trying to be professional, which was admirable to a certain extent. Sex was a distraction, and he didn't want to risk it.

That was okay. The moment this thing was over, he was going to be mine.

~

I woke up in the middle of the night, breathless and terrified.

It was a strange house—not my own—and it took a minute for me to orient myself.

I knew my fear wasn't rational, but I couldn't talk myself out of it, so I got up to go to the bathroom, hoping the distraction would help me relax.

It didn't. So I left the bedroom and went to look for Cole.

He was right outside, sitting on a couch, and he jumped up when he saw me. "Are you okay?"

"Yeah," I assured him, feeling stupid now that I was with him and had caught my breath. "I just woke up and felt kind of... anxious. I'm fine."

I was just wearing a little nightgown, and I saw his eyes slip down a few times to run over my body. I knew he liked what he saw, and it made me a little excited too.

"Do you want me to check your room out?" he asked, clearing his throat.

I shook my head. "No. I didn't think there was anyone there. I just woke up nervous. Thanks though."

He made some sort of sound, but his gaze never left me. I wanted him to say something—anything—but I was getting rather distracted now since his eyes had grown very hot.

"Cole?" I whispered.

"Yeah," he said as he stood up. He was clearly rather distracted too.

I stepped forward, suddenly wanting to feel his body, his strength, his passion. I ran a hand down his chest over his T-shirt.

I heard him grunt, and his whole body grew tense. "We weren't going to do this."

"That was your plan, not mine." I drifted toward him, my nerves from before somehow heightening my response to him now. I raised both arms to wrap around his neck. "If it makes you feel better, we can create some distance between us so this doesn't happen again."

"Right." His hands cupped my bottom, pressing me against him so I could feel his arousal. "Distance."

"We should start distancing ourselves right now."

That was the last thing said before he kissed me.

The kiss was deep and urgent immediately, and it awakened a hunger inside me. Soon I was clawing at him shamelessly, my tongue dueling with his. He lifted me with his hands cupping my ass, and I wrapped my legs around him. He carried me back into the bedroom, and I pulled him down on top of me as soon as he lowered me to the mattress.

We undressed each other hurriedly, the desire too intense to go slow. It was like we were starved for each other, and my mind was a thick, heated blur of need as I ran my hands up and down his smooth back and firm ass.

Then he was rolling on a condom and was settling between my legs.

"Remember," I said breathlessly, bending my legs around his hips. "Don't get too close."

"Right." He slowly pushed himself inside me, my body fitting itself around his length. "Not too close."

He kissed me again, and I held him with my arms and legs, and we built up a fast, pleasing rhythm together, our bodies knowing exactly what they needed from each other. Eventually I broke the kiss, turning my head to the side to suck in air, and Cole started to grunt as his motion got more urgent.

I felt the pleasure deepening, and I arched up into it, my whole body shaking until the pressure finally broke. I cried out and then gasped in satisfaction as I felt him coming too.

We held on to each other afterward, our bodies relaxed and replete, and he pressed little kisses against my neck—which I loved.

They felt tender, as if he still wanted to give a little more.

But the afterglow couldn't last forever, and eventually Cole sat up and seemed to shake himself off, as if he'd remembered who he was and what he was doing here.

"It was bound to happen," I said, heading off whatever he was going to say. "Don't beat yourself up. We both wanted it. It didn't compromise you or anything else."

He gazed at me for a long time. "I'm totally compromised when it comes to you."

He was looking sober, brooding, but I couldn't help but like the sound of those words.

I didn't like the sound of the words he said next though. "It can't happen again."

I told myself not to be disappointed. He was still trying to be professional, but I was sure he wanted me as much as I wanted him. And I was also sure that there was more here than sex.

"Okay," I said with a little smile. "Whatever you say."

It was definitely going to happen again.

The next morning, Sebastian stopped by to talk to me, to see how I was doing.

At least that was what I thought his purpose was until he added, "And just some advice, don't get too close to Cole. It's not a good idea."

My eyebrows arched sky-high. "Excuse me?"

Sebastian's face twisted with some sort of conflicted feeling. "Don't get me wrong... He's a great guy. You know he's one of my best friends. But I see how you're looking at him, and I don't think that would be smart."

I frowned deeply. "Because he's not at my level in some way?"

"Of course not. You know I'm not that sort of snob." He paused. "You don't know him like I do. Cole's a great guy. But he's... he's had a hard life, and he doesn't let himself get close to anyone. Ever. You'll only end up getting hurt."

"I'm a grown-up, Sebastian, and I'm not naive. I can decide who I date, and I can decide who I sleep with."

He looked uncomfortable as he raked a hand through his hair. "Look, I was just trying to help. You're my friend, and I can't help but worry. He's... he's different from you."

"Yeah. Right. He's different."

I was sure Sebastian meant well, but it was very irritating kind of advice to get, so I just walked away from him.

I turned around a corner and almost ran into Cole. I really hoped he hadn't heard the conversation.

TEN
Cole

Three days later, and I was ready to punch something.

Or someone.

Fucking Sebastian.

I heard his conversation with Evangeline the other day, and it took an act of iron will to not haul off and kick his ass right then and there. But I decided to be the bigger person. To let it go. Besides, it wasn't like he had said anything I hadn't already suspected.

That didn't make it hurt any less to actually hear it out loud.

But now? Honestly, I didn't even know why I was here since Seb had been sticking to Evangeline like glue. He claimed he was hanging around to be helpful. He was watching over Evangeline so I could focus on what was going on around the set and get a good look at the list of potential suspects Malcolm and I had finally come up with.

Right.

I believed that as much as I believed in the tooth fairy. Seb was sticking around to make sure I wasn't getting too close to Evangeline or sneaking into her bed.

And believe me, it was a daily battle not to.

The woman was pure temptation. She didn't even have to do anything more than look at me, and I was hard as a rock and ready to throw her over my shoulder and take her to bed.

Which was why I didn't look at her when Sebastian was anywhere nearby. He'd catch that look in a heartbeat, and then I'd have to deal with his bullshit.

Or should I say *more* of his bullshit.

One of the great things about starting the agency with the guys was that we were all independent. I mean, we were partners, but we all worked alone. Sure we'd conference call and occasionally call in to get advice, but for the most part, we each worked our own cases.

Until now.

And it was pretty damn insulting.

The whole reason for my being forced to take this case rather than Sebastian in the first place was because of the conflict of interest angle. Well, what the hell happened to that? Now all of a sudden there was no conflict for him?

Bullshit.

I got it. I wasn't good enough for someone like Evangeline. I came from the wrong side of the tracks. I had a criminal history. I'd been homeless, and I almost killed my own father.

And I killed my best friend.

So yeah, I got it. I could see where Sebastian was coming from. To a point. Over the past two years that we'd been doing this, I had to sit back and listen to him, Levi, and Declan talk about how they had gotten involved with clients, and to be honest, *none* of those were appropriate hookups.

For crying out loud, Harper was Gavin's sister! That alone should have stopped Levi in his tracks. The fact that her life was in danger should have sealed the deal on him keeping his distance. But did he? No.

Ali was a suspect on Sebastian's case. A *suspect!* For all any of us knew, she was some lunatic who was aiming to kill the guy who had essentially ruined her father's life. Yeah, like that was a smart hookup. That had *Fatal Attraction* written all over it.

And Declan? Well, that was just stupid. Don't get me wrong, I thought Kristin was amazing. She was incredibly sweet, and her daughter was cute as hell. But Declan was having a hard enough time keeping his head above water teaching the first grade, and he went and started banging one of his students' moms? What the hell?

The point was, out of the three of them, we all should have been looking out for Harper out of respect for Gavin, and we didn't. Sure, we were all shocked at how Levi was chasing after her, and we razzed the shit out of him on more than one occasion, but none of us stepped in to stop him.

So why me?

Which was exactly what was playing on a constant loop in my head to the point of madness. Evangeline was shooting a scene on location in a grimy downtown park— which was hell to keep secure—and Sebastian was standing right out of camera range. Next to him were two of Malcolm's guys and the director's assistants—Matt and Janelle. Matt was on the top of my list right now because the guy practically salivated when he got within ten feet of Evangeline.

And then there was yesterday's incident.

I still couldn't believe we didn't just haul the kid's ass in and consider ourselves done. Evangeline was shooting a scene, and Seb and Malcolm were both standing watch. I wanted some time to do a little research on some of the names we were narrowed down to. Matt was sitting off by himself—right across from Evangeline's trailer.

And if that wasn't suspicious enough, he was reading. Not that reading was anything to get crazy about, but he was reading a book on animal anatomy.

That piqued my curiosity.

"What are you reading, Matt?" I asked mildly as I approached, but my expression definitely gave away how I was feeling.

The kid looked about ready to wet himself. He scrambled to his feet and held the book behind his back. "Oh... um... I'm... I'm taking some classes at the community college. I... I want to be a veterinarian."

My gaze narrowed, and I stepped in closer. "This is kind of an odd career choice for someone looking to be a pet doctor."

He looked down at his shoes. "Yeah... well... this kind of work is easy for me. I only recently decided to look into veterinary school."

"Can I see the book?"

Matt's eyes were wide when he looked up at me. "See it?"

I nodded. "Yeah. Can I see it? I often wondered about how vets learn all about different animals." I held out my hand and waited. "I'm sure someone who goes through any kind of medical school would have to have a pretty strong stomach. They'd have to cut open animals and deal with blood and guts just like they would with humans."

Matt paled. "I... I suppose."

"Have you ever?"

"Ever what?"

"Cut open an animal?"

Now he was a little green. "N-no. Like I said, I... I just started taking the classes and..."

I heard the director yell *"Cut!"* and before I could say another word, Matt excused himself and ran off toward the set.

Malcolm's only job was to keep an eye on the kid.

There wasn't much going on today for the movie other than this scene, so I knew I could take a few minutes to step away and make a call. I gave my surroundings a final look and walked away to the trailer Malcolm had been using. It was half the size of the one Evangeline has, but it would do.

"Hey, man. What's up? Everything going okay?" Levi asked as soon as he answered the phone.

"Yeah. It's fucking great," I murmured.

"Christ," he sighed. "Now what?"

"I want you to tell Seb to leave."

Silence.

"Levi?"

"I heard you. Okay, tell me why."

"I resent the fact that he's here. I was forced to take this case because he was busy, it was a conflict of interest... and everyone trusted me. Well... clearly none of that's the case anymore because he won't leave. I can't do my fucking job because he's constantly looking over my shoulder and questioning my every move."

"I'm sure it's not..."

"It is." I interrupted. "I'm serious, Levi. I'm tired of this shit. I don't interfere on anyone else's cases. I don't step on anyone's toes, and I certainly don't go around treating you all like a pack of morons or say anything when you're sleeping with someone involved in a case or—"

"Wait, wait, wait," Levi snapped. "You slept with Evangeline?"

Shit. "Not the point, Levi. I'm just saying it's time for Sebastian to leave, or I'm leaving. The two of us aren't needed here. If he thinks he can do a better job and find this psycho, then more power to him. I'll gladly step down. Hell, I'll gladly step down from the company too since I'm clearly too incompetent to do my job."

"Okay, hold on. You're getting ahead of yourself here and not making any sense. You want to quit the company? Since when?"

Yeah, since when? "It's just obvious I'm the weak link here. If it weren't for the Marines, I wouldn't be friends with any of you guys. I'm not like you. And I'm tired of being made to feel like I don't measure up."

"And you came to this conclusion all because Sebastian is helping with a friend?" he asked flatly.

"Partly. I've known it for a long time. I just think it might be best for everyone if Seb just officially took over here, and once we go to DC and hear the findings on Gavin, I just go out on my own."

He made a noncommittal sound, and then I heard the baby crying in the background. For a minute Levi must have put the phone down because I heard him talking softly to Harper before coming back on the line. "Sorry about that."

"Not a big deal."

"Um... here's the thing. No."

"What? What do you mean 'no'?"

"I think you need to get your panties out of their knot and quit pouting. No one thinks you're incompetent, and no one thinks they're better than you. And that shit about us not being friends if it weren't for the Marines is bullshit. I think you're using some sort of reverse snobbery here, and you know what? Now I'm insulted. How do you like that?"

"Seriously? That's your theory?"

"It's no more ridiculous than yours," Levi countered.

"Just... just get him to leave. If you truly trust me... if *all* of you trust me... then get him to leave."

"Cole, seriously man, his being there is more out of some sort of misplaced sense of obligation to his family. It's not about you. It's about—"

"Then I'm done," I snapped. "I'm... I'm just done, Levi. There's my offer. Take it or leave it, but if Sebastian stays, I'm leaving. He can work with Malcolm. We finally have a decent list of suspects, and he can just take over."

"Dammit! You're not being reasonable! This is business, Cole. You can't take this shit personally. You just need to..."

"Did any of us come and check up on you when you were protecting Harper?"

"What?"

"You heard me."

"What does that have to do with anything?"

"I'm just saying... she's Gavin's sister. We all knew her. Her life was in danger too. Did we all come around and set up camp in your living room and make sure you were doing your job and keeping your hands to yourself?"

"Is that really what this is all about? You're pissed because Sebastian is cock-blocking you?"

"You don't know what you're talking about!"

"Are you sure that *you* know what you're talking about anymore?" Levi stopped and sighed loudly. "Look, if you want Sebastian gone, I'll make the call."

"Thank you."

"Under one condition."

"*Motherfucker*," I hissed under my breath.

"There's no more talk of you leaving the company. We're friends, Cole. More than that. We're brothers. All of us. Got it?"

My chest tightened. How many times had we all said that to one another when we were deployed and missing our families, our friends, our lives back home? "Yeah," I said quietly. "I got it."

"Okay then. Good." He paused. "And for the record, Cole? I get what you're saying. Back when it was me and Harper? It was wrong for me to sleep with her while she was under my protection." He gave a small chuckle. "The only problem was that it was completely out of my control. I couldn't deny my feelings for her. And if you or Seb or Declan had stepped in and tried to interfere? Well, I probably would have put up one hell of a fight. Sort of like what you're doing now."

"Look, it's not just about sleeping with Evangeline."

Levi chuckled again. "You keep telling yourself that. Yeah, Seb's there when he said he wouldn't or couldn't be. But the reality is that he could be a real help to the case."

"All he's doing is standing guard. He's not talking to anyone—except Evangeline—and he's not helping me or Malcolm with squat."

"Ah, so he really is just there to cock-block you," he said and laughed again. "I'll make the call, Cole. You've got my word on that. But do us both a favor?"

"What?"

"If you're just looking to get laid to pass the time, find someone else to do it with, and stop complicating this case."

"I'm not—"

"But if you're really into her," Levi continued, ignoring my words, "then explain that to Sebastian so he can leave with a clear conscience. Please. Can you do that?"

"Can you guarantee he's not going to come at me like I'm some low-life degenerate who isn't good enough to lay a hand on his friend?"

Another laugh. "I'm not sure I can guarantee that, but I'll see what I can do."

He hung up before I could argue with him any further.

~

"Dude! What the hell?"

I looked up from the notes I was making while Malcolm and I went over the events of the day to find Sebastian angrily staring down at me. "Problem?"

Malcolm nervously looked between the two of us and quickly made an excuse and walked out.

"Yeah, problem," Sebastian said snidely. "You called Levi? You threatened to quit if I didn't leave? Seriously? What is your fucking problem?"

"You!" I snapped as I stood up and kicked my chair out from behind me and came around the table at him. "You're my problem! I thought that was obvious!"

"Why? I'm here, and I'm trying to help! Why is that a bad thing all of a sudden?"

"If you wanted to handle the case, why didn't you from the beginning? You gave me that whole line of bullshit that you were going away with Ali, it's a conflict of interest, and now all of a sudden, you're free as a bird! We've never worked as partners on any case before—none of us! —and suddenly here you are. Well I'm tired of it. Either take over the case or leave!"

He glared at me long and hard, and for a minute I thought he was going to rear back and punch me.

Then I remembered who I was dealing with. Prettyboy Sebastian didn't do that sort of thing. It wasn't dignified. Only white trash like me gets into fistfights I guess.

Sebastian sighed. "Can't you understand where I'm coming from? We're friends. Just like you and I are friends. If it was you who was in danger, I'd want to be there too."

"You're full of it. You know that, right?"

He looked at me quizzically. "What are you talking about?"

"You weren't concerned enough to be here until you thought I was sleeping with her. Then all of a sudden your schedule cleared up. Tell me, is Ali okay with you being here, hovering around your movie-star friend?"

"Please, don't try to use that sort of nonsense on me. Ali knows exactly who Eva is and what she is to me. She's even met her a couple of times. Don't try to plant the jealousy seed because it's an embarrassment to us both." He raked a hand through his hair. "Just answer one question for me, and then I swear I'll never bring it up again."

I had a sinking feeling in my gut that I knew what he was going to ask, but I simply nodded and waited.

"Do you really have feelings for her, or are you just fucking around?"

Man, I hated to have to have this conversation with him. And I hated that I was going to have to admit out loud to him something I was having trouble comprehending myself. I cleared my throat. "I'm not... I mean... she means something."

Sebastian stared hard at me for a long time before giving me a curt nod.

I wasn't sure what we were supposed to do just then—shake hands? Hug? I mean, it was only one question, and I gave a relatively short answer, but it felt like it all held a lot more weight than that.

"So," he began, "are we good?"

Were we? I still didn't want him here. I wanted him gone. I wanted to figure out who was stalking Evangeline so I could stop being her bodyguard. I wanted...

Her. I just wanted her.

He was still studying me—waiting for an answer. I was just about to reach out a hand to him when there was a scream and a loud crash from outside the trailer. We both cursed and bolted for the door. Malcolm went racing by, and it hit me—who the hell had been watching Evangeline?

Malcolm got to her trailer first, and Sebastian beat me by a few seconds, but by the time I stepped in the door, I was ready to kill. I scanned the room and saw that Malcolm was looking at some photos that were positioned on the makeshift kitchen table.

"What happened?" I asked, my voice gruff.

I expected someone to answer me. No, that wasn't right. I expected Evangeline to come to me and answer me. But she didn't. She took one look at Sebastian and burst into tears and then threw herself into his arms.

For a brief moment, the case was all but forgotten because the shock and rage I felt at seeing Evangeline in Sebastian's arms nearly blinded me. Never in my life had I felt this... this... jealous. I never get close to anyone—not even my friends—and yet somehow in a matter of weeks, Evangeline had become so important to me, so vital, that I was actually contemplating killing one of my best friends because he was comforting her.

Mentally I shook myself out of my stupor and walked over to Malcolm. "What have we got?" He motioned to the photos. All of them were of Evangeline—all of them taken off the set. There were even a few taken at Sebastian's family estate when we were coming and going. All taken with a high-powered camera lens.

And all had various threats written on them in red marker.

"This just got worse, didn't it?" Malcolm asked, and I nodded. He lowered his voice as he pulled me farther away from where Seb and Evangeline were still standing. "This means all our decoys and changing how and where we drive isn't working, Cole. Whoever this is has got to be here on the set. Someone closer than we've thought."

Suddenly I remembered Evangeline mentioning how she thought Malcolm had been acting odd. I studied him hard for a long moment—until he visibly started to squirm under my scrutiny.

"What? What are you thinking?"

My emotions were too close to the surface, and I said exactly what I was thinking. "I think it's you."

"What?" he hissed. "Are you fucking kidding me? Why? Why would you even think that?"

"What do you expect me to think?" I backed him into a corner but kept my voice low. "You and I are the only ones who have constant access to her. Hell, we don't even tell most of your team what we have planned. So since it's not me—because this shit started long before I ever got here—that only leaves you, Malcolm."

His eyes grew wide for a second before he shoved me—hard—and came at me. "You arrogant son of a bitch. Do you even hear yourself?"

I wanted to fight. Hell, nothing would give me more pleasure than to unleash all the rage I had in me on Malcolm right here, right now. I looked over my shoulder toward Sebastian. "Get her out of here. *Now.*" My tone left no room for argument, and I was glad that he simply complied and led her out of the trailer.

Then I turned my attention back to Malcolm. "Yeah. I hear myself, and I can't believe we're even going to have this conversation. And yet… here we are."

"Cole, I'm telling you… it's not me. I swear," Malcolm said, his voice earnest and sincere. "I don't care if you believe me or not, but I'm telling you, it's not me!"

"Then explain this! Explain how it's possible that you're the only one who could have known where we were in all these pictures!"

He looked like he was about to argue, but then his posture became defeated. "I... I can't. I wish to hell that I could, Cole. I've been with Evangeline for so long... Why would you think I'd want to scare her? I spend my life trying to protect her!"

"Maybe you're trying to prove that you're actually needed. Maybe guarding a former teen idol was getting boring for you. You've gotten lazy. Maybe you heard a rumor that you were going to be replaced, and you needed to do something to show that you could still do something around here."

His eyes narrowed at me. "You know, I'm getting a little tired of you putting me down all the damn time. I have done everything you've asked me to do—even more—and yet you still talk to me like I'm some sort of rent-a-cop!"

"Prove me wrong," I snapped. "Seriously, dude, fucking prove me wrong! If you didn't take these pictures, who did?"

"Isn't that your job?" he asked snidely.

I saw red. I was trembling from head to toe with the need to just pound him into the pavement, so I took my shot. I reached out and swung, and my fist hit what felt like concrete in his jaw. He immediately swung back, and before I knew it, furniture was flying and we were on the ground.

"What the fuck!" Sebastian yelled as he came back into the room. He ran over and pulled Malcolm and I apart. "That's enough! This is not helping anything!" He shoved Malcolm in one direction and me in another.

"Where's Evangeline?" I demanded.

"She's in Pete's office with Cali. I've got a guard stationed right outside the door. No one is allowed in or out unless I tell him."

Fucking great. Now Sebastian was in control.

My jaw and my ribs hurt like hell, and I could feel some swelling near my eye. Just what I needed on top of everything else.

"What were you two thinking?" Sebastian asked, looking between us.

"I think Malcolm is our stalker," I said.

"*What?*" Sebastian looked at me like I was crazy. "Why?"

I gave him my theory, and for a minute there, I thought he was going to back me up. Then he turned to Malcolm. "Did you do this?"

"No."

"Then prove it," Seb said.

"How? How the hell am I supposed to do that?"

"You're suspended. You and you're entire team. I want you all off the set until this case is solved. As soon as it is, you'll be back as Evangeline's bodyguard—if she wants you to—but until then, you and your guys collect your things, get off the set, and stay away from it until either Cole or I call you. If I see even one of your guys snooping around, I'll have all of you arrested for harassment. Do I make myself clear?"

I wanted to throw my two cents in, but basically, Seb had nailed it. It was exactly what I would do—had I been thinking clearly. I looked over at Malcolm, expecting some kind of argument from him, but he simply nodded and began collecting his things. He pulled a business card out of his wallet and handed it to Sebastian.

And then he was gone.

When the door closed and it was just the two of us, Sebastian studied me. Hard. "Are you all right?"

"Yeah." I rubbed my jaw a little. "I really... I thought it was him. Evangeline mentioned how weird he'd been acting and..."

"I know. She mentioned that once I got her out of here."

"Is she all right?"

He shook his head. "No. She's asking for you."

I froze. "Why?"

He chuckled softly. "Hell if I know. Look, I want you to go and be with her. I'm going to work on getting a new team out here ASAP. Once they're all in place, I'll meet up with you back at the house. I'll also make sure to beef up security there too."

"I can do something, you know," I said defensively.

Seb said wearily. "I think you're wound up right now, and maybe you need a little time to cool off."

"Whatever," I muttered.

"Now what? What the hell have I done now?"

I turned to leave, but then without looking over my shoulder, I said, "She went to you first."

"What?"

"You. When we all came in here to see what happened, she went to you."

"So?"

I paused and felt more than a little deflated. "Never mind."

I walked out of the trailer and made my way to where Evangeline was. But the scene continued to play out in my head. There were three of us there with her, and she chose to go to Sebastian. Didn't that really say it all? Here I was tormenting myself and agonizing over the fact that I wanted her—needed her—so damn much, but at the end of the day, she was no different than anyone else. I was beneath her. I was always going to be beneath her.

I wasn't good enough.

Not as a lover.

Not as a bodyguard.

I arrived at the trailer and saw the guard on his phone. "Yes, sir. He just got here," he said. "Okay. Thanks." He placed his phone back in his pocket. "Mr. Maxwell said you can go in."

Like the cherry on a fucking sundae. Yippy for me. Seb said I can do my job.

Rather than be a dick to the guard, I nodded and walked up the steps and let myself in. Evangeline and Cali were sitting on the sofa. Evangeline's head was on Cali's shoulder. I knew instantly that she was still shaking.

Lifting her head, Evangeline looked at me and gasped. "Oh my God! What happened? Did you... did you catch him? The person who took the pictures?"

I shook my head and looked at Cali. "You can go. I'm going to take her back to the house."

"Are you sure?" Cali asked. "Isn't there someplace else you can go?"

"It's still the safest place for now," I said, my voice flat and emotionless. She finally stood and wished us both a goodnight before leaving.

"I don't know if I can go back there," Evangeline said quietly. "I mean, whoever this is, they know where I am."

I nodded. "But they won't get in. Sebastian is bringing in more security, and Malcolm's entire team is being replaced."

"What? Why?"

"It's none of your concern," I said firmly. "Let's go."

"But—"

"Now, Clementine," I added snarkily.

Her eyes narrowed at me as she stood up. "We're back to that?"

"We never should have left it." Then I called Seb to find out where the car was and had the guard walk with us to escort her there.

The drive back was spent in silence. Well, she was silent. I was on the phone with Sebastian and then Levi and Declan to go over who the new team was that was coming in and what high-tech devices we were finally going to bring in to plant around the set. The movie studio and the director were not on board with us putting up surveillance equipment in the beginning. They thought it would somehow leak to the media, and they didn't want any scenes getting out.

They were singing a different tune now.

By the time we'd arrived back at the house, I was pretty sure Evangeline was a little more relaxed, but I was still on edge. We went inside, and I secured every room and made sure every window was covered.

"We're clear," I said to her when I was done.

"Cole... I... I wanted to... I need..."

"Go to bed, Angelina," I murmured. "Just... go."

"Can't we at least talk? I mean, this is my life we're dealing with. I have the right to know what's going on!"

She had a point, but at the moment, I was all talked out. "You heard me on the phone while we were driving here. What more do you want?"

"How about a little kindness? A little sympathy?"

"Sorry, princess. I'm fresh out of that crap." I stalked to the kitchen and began to make myself a sandwich. I knew she followed me in, but I was serious. I didn't want to talk, and sympathy was the last thing on my mind.

I didn't offer to make her something to eat. I didn't pour her a drink when I got one for myself. I acted as if I was in the room completely by myself.

Yeah, I was a piece of crap. What else is new?

"Why are you being like this?" she finally asked, her voice cracking with emotion.

"Just here to do my job, Your Highness. That's all." I put all the food away and turned and gave her a mock salute. "Sebastian will be here later. I'm sure you'll wait up for him." I grabbed my plate and glass and left the room.

It was too much to hope that she'd just let me go. I was halfway to my room when she called my name. I stopped, but I didn't turn around.

"What am I supposed to do?" she asked quietly.

"Go to your room. Grab a sandwich. Hell, watch some TV. You're safe in here. No one's getting in. Just don't open the curtains or the blinds." And then I continued to walk away.

"Aren't you supposed to stay with me?"

"I'm entitled to a fucking break," I snapped. And then I was done listening. I was done talking.

I was done caring.

As soon as I got to my room, I stepped in and slammed the door.

And cursed Evangeline to hell for making me feel like this.

ELEVEN
Evangeline

I really wished Sebastian was staying with me tonight instead of Cole.

I didn't feel safer with him—nothing felt as safe to me as Cole's rough, hard presence—but things were easier with Sebastian.

He felt familiar and calm. He didn't stir up all these feelings and emotions like Cole did.

Right now anger was the primary emotion I was feeling.

He'd always been unpredictable, swinging from cold rudeness to hot tenderness with the turn of a moment. But he seemed to have suddenly jumped back in time to the beginning of our relationship when he didn't know or like me at all.

He *did* know me. He *did* like me. I was absolutely sure of it. Which made his behavior this afternoon all the more maddening.

I was scared enough after seeing those photos. I didn't need to deal with this too.

Thick-skulled, insensitive ass.

I'd been soaking in a bubble bath for twenty minutes, sipping a glass of red wine and thinking angsty thoughts. About the stalker, who seemed to be getting closer to me by the day.

And about Cole.

Finally, when my attempt to relax and clear my head was obviously a failed effort, I stepped out of the tub, drained the water, and toweled off.

If Cole hadn't crawled out of his hole when I came out of my bedroom, I was going to call up Sebastian and demand I get a bodyguard who was willing to do his job.

I could be getting killed in here, for all Cole knew or cared.

Simmering with righteous resentment, I threw on a little satin robe and walked out of my bedroom to the sitting room outside my door where Cole was normally stationed.

He was there. Staring out the window into the night. Brooding.

"If I'd known I was getting Heathcliff as a bodyguard," I snapped, "I would have reconsidered."

He turned slowly, unsurprised. He'd obviously known I was standing behind him. It was really hard to catch a man like Cole unaware. "And I guess you think I don't even know who Heathcliff is."

He sounded so bitter it stung, and I took a step backward. "I don't care if you know who Heathcliff is. I'm saying you're *acting* like him—that kind of selfish, vindictive, irrational brooding that accomplishes nothing. So tell me what the hell is wrong with you! What happened today?"

"Nothing happened."

I was so angry now at his obstinacy that I stepped forward until I was right in front of him, close enough to touch. But I didn't. "Don't lie to me. We made love a few days ago, and now you're acting like we're strangers."

As soon as I'd said the words, I wished I could pull them back. I couldn't believe I'd said "made love" like that. It sounded silly, sentimental, melodramatic—when nothing about a serious relationship had ever been spoken between us.

I knew he'd take the words wrong, and he did. His head snapped up with a cold glare. "We fucked a couple of times. That doesn't mean we're anything but strangers."

And that was painful too. Very painful. Because I knew we weren't strangers. I knew the times we'd spent together meant more than just empty sex. "You don't mean that," I said, the words strangling a little in my throat. "You're angry for some reason and trying to push me away, but you don't mean that."

He gave his head a little shake. "I'm sorry if you thought there was more, but all we had going for us was sex. And now we don't even have that."

The words were like blows, and I turned away from him in the brunt of them. I started to leave so he wouldn't see me cry, but then I thought about how he'd looked at me when we'd been having sex the other night.

He was lying to me now. Lying right to my face.

I sucked in a breath and whirled around. "You can say that as much as you want, but I don't believe you. I don't know what happened or why you think we can't be together, but I'm not prepared to accept that. We have something good. Something better than I've had in…" The words trailed off as I was hit with a revelation that left me breathless. "Ever."

That got a reaction from him. He sucked in a sharp, audible breath, and he glanced away. His big body was tense with some sort of coiled energy.

I reached out—unable to resist—and put a hand on his chest.

He took a quick step back, his face growing cold again. "You got it all wrong," he gritted out. "But the sex was good. Thanks for that."

It felt like he slapped me. "Damn it, Cole, why are you—"

"Enough!" His rough tone immediately silenced me. "I'm here to do my job, and that's all. I'd suggest you go back to your room, unless you came out here wearing practically nothing hoping to get laid. I'm happy to oblige. It's as good a way as any to pass the time."

The words were cold, heartless, and the worst thing was I knew they weren't sincere.

I wasn't convinced by this cold, cruel person he was trying to be.

But I knew enough to know he wasn't going to budge on this. Not now anyway.

Maybe never.

I might have to resign myself to never getting what I wanted from him.

To never getting *him*.

It was a brutal thought, and I was fighting tears as I returned to my bedroom without another word.

I made sure not to let him see though.

A girl's got to have her pride, even when her heart's been broken.

~

I didn't get much sleep that night, but it was more from stewing about Cole than from worries about the stalker.

While I was in the Maxwell house with all its security and with Cole right outside my door, I felt safe.

As soon as I left the house the next morning, though, my fear kicked up into overdrive.

I was chilled with anxiety as the driver took us to the studio. It felt like there was a threat around every corner, lurking at every stoplight.

Cole was tense and silent, but I was too distracted to really focus on him.

I was used to being in the public eye. I'd lived that way most of my life. But being hunted like this was different. I felt exposed in a way I never had before.

I hated the feeling. Hated it. Desperately wanted it to end.

I made a mess of my morning scenes at the park. I performed the lines and stood in the right places and did all the correct actions, but even I could tell there was no heart to my acting. I was as wooden as I'd ever been.

I was a professional. I'd done my job when I was going through breakups, when a friend died, when I was dealing with a flurry of negative publicity. I'd always been able to put it aside and focus on the scene at hand though.

Not today.

I was mortified and upset when the director finally called a break, saying we'd try again in an hour.

I knew Cole had been watching the whole time, and I didn't want to know what he'd been thinking about me.

He walked me back to my trailer, making me wait outside while he carefully searched the interior—even though a big, rough-looking guy had been standing guard at the door the whole time.

When he'd determined it was clear, he waved me in.

I sat down on the couch and hugged myself, telling myself to get it together.

So someone was stalking me. So Cole didn't want me.

It didn't mean my life was over.

"I'm going to catch him," Cole murmured after a minute.

He'd been watching me. Probably felt sorry for me. Evidently, my pitifulness had broken through even his thick, stubborn exterior.

"I know."

"We've made progress. We're closing in. I know it doesn't seem like we're getting anywhere, but we are."

I wasn't looking at him. "I know."

I was shaking now and trying to hold the trembling back by tightening my arms around my middle.

I hated being like this. I wished the past month could just start over.

Cole made a rough sound in his throat and sat down beside me, pulling me into the protection of his arms.

I broke down a little, shaking against him, taking comfort in who he was—even though he was part of the reason I was such a mess.

I could feel emotion in his embrace. I could sense real, deep feeling. He was holding me like I was precious, like he needed me, like he wanted nothing more in the world.

And suddenly I knew it was true.

I pulled back just enough to look up in his face. "Cole, I need you," I admitted.

His face twisted briefly. "I know. I'm going to keep you safe. I promise."

Shaking my head, I said, "I mean more than that. I need all of you. Even after the stalker is caught."

He jerked his face to the side. "Evangeline, I can't—"

"Yes, you can. I don't know why you've gotten it into your head that we can't be together. I don't know why you're so convinced that you're somehow not good enough for me. But it's nonsense. It's lies that you're telling yourself. I really think we belong together."

The words came spilling out, the deepest expression of my heart, but I didn't regret them. I knew they were true. I knew they were right.

But Cole released me and stood up, slightly awkwardly. He wasn't looking me in the eyes. "I don't think so. It's a different man you want, a different man you need."

And those words were final. I knew it. And the hope I'd been holding on to died a sudden death.

I was numb with it. Had no idea what to say, what to do. I stared up at him blankly and hoped the world would turn enough to make sense again, not hurt this way.

He stared back at me for a long, thick moment and then turned his back to me with a guttural sound.

He was reaching for the door when there was a tap on it.

Matt was standing outside the door, a sheaf of papers in his hand. "I have some notes on the scene from the director."

"I'll take them." Cole blocked the entrance and grabbed the papers from the younger man.

"But...," Matt began.

Cole handed me the papers and then stepped outside, keeping Matt from coming in.

I wondered again if Matt was the stalker. He was kind of strange and quiet. He seemed to have a weird crush on me.

It was possible. It would make sense.

I just wished Cole would get proof so this whole thing could be over.

There was another tap on the door before I could start to read the notes. Cole stuck his head in. "Janelle is coming in here with a message from Pete. I'm not letting Matt in."

"Okay."

I could well imagine what the director wanted to tell me. Get it together, or he'd have to find another star for his film.

Janelle came in with a friendly smile. "Sorry to bother you."

"It's fine." I smiled back at her politely and relaxed against the back of the couch.

"Everyone is all suspicious of Matt all of a sudden, but I think he seems pretty harmless. He just has the hots for you, is all."

"Sometimes people seem harmless when they aren't."

"I guess so. Anyway, the director was kind of concerned this morning, but I told him you were dealing with a lot, so he should give you a little time."

"Thanks," I said. "I'm sure I can get it together soon." It was nice that Janelle was being sympathetic, but I really wanted to get the message and then be alone for a little while so I could have a good cry.

"I think you've been great." She had the same gushing admiration she always did, but I really wasn't up to it this morning. "All that stuff you're dealing with, and you haven't broken down."

I had kind of broken down, but she wouldn't know that.

I cleared my throat, suddenly unable to deal with this girl in my trailer. "Anyway, did he have anything else to say?"

Something almost palpable cracked on her face, her smile. "What?"

"The director? You said there was a message?"

"Are you trying to get rid of me?" There was a new note in her voice now. Shrill. A little too much to be a reasonable response to what I'd just said.

Shit. I'd offended her somehow, even though I was doing my best to be polite. "I'm sorry. I'm just really tired and need a little downtime on my own."

"Of course you do."

I opened my eyes at her brittle tone. "What?"

"Of course you need some downtime. Of course you need to be alone even if it means slamming the door in the face of other people." Janelle sounded bitter and ice cold, and it was so shocking I felt a shudder of cold anxiety run through me.

The transformation was so surprising I couldn't process it immediately. "What are you talking about?"

"I'm talking about you. Always the center of attention. Everyone catering to your every whim. Treating you like you're something special. All the way back to when you were twelve."

"When I was twelve?"

"I bet you don't even know. Don't even remember, do you?" Something new was growing on Janelle's face, a kind of wildness, an irrationality that was utterly frightening. "I bet you don't even remember me. I auditioned for the role of Emma too."

Emma was the first role I played on the cable show. It had made my name, and I'd been fighting the stereotype for my entire career.

"You did?" I breathed, trying to catch up, even as my heart was pounding with growing fear in my chest, my throat, my hands.

"Yes, I did. But of course you got it instead of me. I was just as good as you. I could sing. I could dance. But it didn't matter. You always get what you want, don't you? Everyone always bows and flatters and gives you whatever you want. When it should have been *me*!"

My brain finally started to work, even through the chaos of shock and fear I was experiencing. Janelle was the stalker. Not Matt. Not some crazed boy with a crush.

And I was alone in my trailer with her.

Cole had let her in, thinking it was a safety precaution.

I started very slowly to stand up.

"Don't you dare move," she hissed, pulling something out of her pocket.

It was a flat black object about the size of a credit card, but she unfolded it to reveal a scary-looking knife.

I froze, on my feet but not quite straightened up.

"It's time someone gave you what you really deserve." Her voice was cold, her eyes a little crazed. "You take and you take and you take! And everyone is too stupid to realize that you're nothing special."

My hands were shaking helplessly, and my legs felt ice cold. It was surreal, so bizarre. The world didn't work this way. Perfectly nice girls didn't turn into unhinged stalkers this way in the matter of two minutes.

"I'm sorry," I managed to say, vaguely hoping I could calm her down until Cole came in.

Surely he'd come in here soon. He'd notice that Janelle wasn't leaving.

"I'm sorry if I ever did anything to hurt you."

"You did, but you're not sorry. You never even *knew* I existed. When you stole my role, my career. My life! That role meant everything to me! It was my chance to finally be somebody! It was finally going to be my time to show my parents that I wasn't useless. I was going to prove to everyone that I was special! I should be you!" She took a few steps closer to me, brandishing the knife.

She was going to kill me. Right here in the trailer, with Cole right outside standing guard.

I could see it in her eyes. I knew it was true.

If I didn't do something right now, she would do it.

I opened my mouth, but the knife was suddenly at my throat. "Here's a little direction for you, *Emma*. If you make a sound, I'll kill you."

She was going to do it anyway. She'd lost whatever touch with reality she'd ever had. She would kill me if I screamed, and she would kill me if I didn't scream.

Cole wouldn't get in here quick enough either way.

I took a step backward and felt a vase of flowers behind my hand—Jimmy had sent them to me a couple of days ago.

With a flick of my hand, I knocked them over, hoping for a crash that would alert Cole and distract Janelle.

The knife was too close to my throat now to try to fight her off. I'd never get an arm or leg up in time.

The vase toppled slowly and then turned over on its side. It made a noise but not a very loud one.

The flowers kept the vase from rolling off to the floor, where it would have made a much louder sound.

Janelle didn't even seem to have noticed it.

"When you're gone," she was saying, her eyes crazed, almost inhuman, "then I'll get my career back. Pete will cast me to replace you. I've been practicing all of the lines, and I know exactly what to do. And then all of this—the dressing room, the assistants, the money and fame, will all be mine. Just like it should have been."

The trailer door suddenly swung open. "Evangeline," Cole said, "are you—"

He took in the scene in about two seconds and was across the trailer before either Janelle or I could react. He moved so quickly that I could have imagined it.

He tackled her, pulling her arm down before she could make a slash toward my throat.

I stumbled back instinctively, as far from her as possible. I bumped into the wall and lost my balance, ending up on the floor.

Janelle was screaming obscenities at him and thrashing now, but Cole had her in a wrestler's hold so she couldn't move or raise her arms.

Two other members of security came running in too, and then they were hauling Janelle out of the room. There was a lot of commotion outside the trailer. People were yelling and asking questions.

And I totally lost it. The world just wasn't working the way it was supposed to. Everything had turned painfully inside out and upside down.

I burst into embarrassing tears, still huddled on the floor where I'd fallen.

Cole had been snapping out orders to the guys who had taken Janelle outside, but he turned around when he heard me. He slammed the door closed.

Then he was there on the floor beside me, pulling me into his arms, holding me as tightly as he'd held me before.

And he was murmuring, "It's okay. I've got you. It's over now. You're safe."

But I could feel the rapid beat of his heart and how his body was trembling almost as much as mine.

For some reason, it was reassuring.

"You're going to be okay," he said softly.

After a few minutes, I believed him.

This hadn't changed everything. The world wasn't all set to rights again. Even now I was sure that Cole hadn't changed his mind about me.

But at least I had an answer. At least this one part was over.

At least I was safe and, for the moment, wrapped in Cole's arms.

TWELVE
Cole

I was back in uniform.

I was standing at attention.

All around me, people were talking, but I couldn't hear a damn thing.

My heart was pounding so loudly in my brain that it was all I could do to just remember to breathe. In a matter of minutes, I knew my life was going to change.

For the worse.

By the time our CO finished reading the report in his hands, I was going to lose everything—my friends, my career, the life that I'd built for myself.

And I'd completely deserve it.

It would almost be a relief to have it all be over.

I was so focused on a spot on the wall—anything to keep me from actually having to engage in conversation with anyone—that I didn't immediately realize we'd been asked to sit. Levi nudged me discreetly and motioned for me to take a seat. I was almost thankful to do so since my legs felt as if they were about to give out.

The CO was talking again, but in my mind, it was muffled. My throat was dry, and I felt like I was going to be sick.

I needed to focus, to listen. I needed to hear it for myself—to know that what they'd found just proved what

I've known all along—that Gavin would be alive right now if it wasn't for me.

I looked over at Levi and realized that I cost his wife her brother—and her parents, their son. He'd never want anything to do with me ever again after this. Even if no formal charges were ever brought against me, I'd be nothing more than a horrible reminder of everything I cost his family.

Levi had been a good friend. One of the best. I wouldn't make it hard for him—or for Harper. I'd just sell my share of the company and just... go away.

It would be for the best.

Declan and Sebastian would probably wash their hands of me as well. How could they not? They'd pretend we were all fine—probably even try to convince me that someday Levi and Harper would forgive me. But it wouldn't matter. These three guys... they were the best thing that had ever happened to me. When I met them in boot camp, my life was a mess. I never had any real friends—had never known what it was like to have people who really cared about me. A family.

And now I was going to lose them and go back to where I belonged.

Alone.

On my own.

With no one to give a damn if I was dead or alive.

My brain immediately conjured up Evangeline's face. I knew that, somewhere inside her, she actually believed we could be something together, but once Sebastian told her about what the report had found, she'd be thankful that I walked away. After all, it wouldn't look good for one of

Hollywood's biggest actresses to be linked to a guy who got his best friend killed.

It would be too much for any tabloid magazine.

I must have missed more than I thought because suddenly I was hearing, "And in conclusion," and my heart just stopped. I felt myself leaning forward. Waiting.

"...it is found that through all our investigation—interviews and eyewitness accounts—that Gunnery Sergeant Gavin Murphy rushed the orders and in doing such, moved into an area that hadn't been cleared or secured."

What?

If I wasn't mistaken, the CO was a little choked up by the news. He placed the report down on the podium and looked at the four of us. "He was a good man," he said solemnly. "I know I don't have to tell any of you that. What happened was a tragedy. An accident. The United States Marine Corp was proud to call Gavin Murphy one of our own." And with little more than a nod of his head, he exited the room.

Not one of us moved.

I couldn't speak for Sebastian, Declan, or Levi, but I still felt like I was going to be sick. I knew I heard what the report said, and I knew I should be relieved... but I wasn't. Basically, the report cleared me of any wrongdoing. But it was just as hard to deal with the fact that there was no one to blame for Gavin's death.

It would have given me closure.

It would have given all of us closure.

Sebastian stood and raked a hand through his hair. I watched him pace silently back and forth a couple of times, and I could see the same restlessness in him I knew I was feeling. It didn't take long for Declan to stand and then Levi.

He was the one I was worried about the most. He had to go and tell Harper and her parents what the report had found.

I refused to say that Gavin was to blame. I couldn't. Gavin was passionate about what he was doing, and deep down to the very bottom of my soul, I refused to lay blame on him. He paid the ultimate price. Wasn't that enough?

"I've got to go and call Harper," Levi said quietly. "I'll meet you all outside."

I watched him go, and honestly, I wished the news was different. I wished for Harper's sake that there was a face to put on this tragedy that wasn't her brother's. I'd gladly take the responsibility all on myself just to give her and her family a different outcome. And peace.

But I couldn't.

I was numb. I was expecting a different outcome, and now I didn't know what to do with myself. I didn't feel any joy. I didn't feel any relief. I just felt… nothing.

It was easy to believe that I had screwed up. That was my life's story. It was what I'd always been told and what I'd always lived up to. But for once, when it really mattered, I didn't screw up.

"Hey," Declan said, sitting back down beside me. "You okay?"

I looked at him for a long moment—as if seeing him for the first time. He said my name, and suddenly it hit me. "Yeah," I said. "Yeah, I am."

And I actually believed it.

It was a familiar scene—the four of us sitting around a table at a bar. We'd been doing it for years. The drive over was spent in silence, and even though no one asked where we were going, Sebastian—who was driving—seemed to know exactly where we needed to go.

"Someone please say something," Declan finally said. "I… I can't stand the silence anymore. I mean, that was some pretty heavy shit we heard today. How could we not have something to say about it?"

"What is there to say?" Seb asked. "It was all right there in black-and-white."

Another long silence. Each of us seemed lost in our own thoughts as we drank our beers, our whisky, our gin.

"I thought I killed him," Levi said lowly.

"What?" we all asked collectively.

He looked up, his expression bleak. "All this time"—his voice clogged with emotion— "I thought I was responsible for killing him." He paused. "There were times I couldn't even look at my wife, my in-laws, because I was so riddled with guilt. All I could think of was how they were going to hate me when it was proved that I was responsible. As it was, I couldn't help but imagine that every time they looked at me that they were wishing I had been the one to die rather than Gavin."

"How could you even think that?" Seb asked. "You were… You always…" He seemed to struggle to find the right words before he finally sighed. "I thought it was me."

"You? How?" Levi asked. "I was in charge. I was the one…"

"I wasn't paying attention. Or at least I thought I wasn't paying attention. All this time I kept wondering what I'd missed or what I could have said to stop him…"

Declan gave a mirthless laugh. "That about sums up how I was feeling too." He looked at the three of us sadly and shrugged. "We all know that I'm the slacker of the group. You guys were always picking up after me. I've been replaying that day in my mind all this time—trying to figure out what I didn't see. I remember thinking that the whole exercise was a bust. That there wasn't a threat. If I had taken it a little more seriously…"

"I was next to him," I finally said, my voice raw. "I saw everything he saw, and I never saw it coming. I heard the order, but when I turned to look at Gavin… he was gone. He had moved. I… I thought I heard the order wrong. That we were supposed to move. I was getting up and then…" My voice trailed off, and I took a moment to just breathe. "I thought I had missed something, and because I hadn't moved when Gavin had that I'd… That it was my fault… and…"

"Fuck," Declan muttered, scrubbing a hand over his face. "Why haven't we ever talked about this? It's been two damn years; why are we all just sharing this now?"

"Why didn't you share it?" I snapped.

He looked away, uncomfortable. "I… I didn't want anyone to… I thought you'd all…"

"Yeah," Seb said. "We know. Because we're all guilty of the same damn thing. We all felt responsible and didn't know what the hell to do about it. Who the fuck wants to admit that they were responsible for someone's death? Especially when that someone is like a damn brother to you?"

"So what do we do now?" Declan asked.

"I don't feel...," I began and then cleared my throat. "I don't feel... absolved. There's a part of me that still feels responsible. Like I wasn't watching his back. I should have pulled him back when he moved. If I was paying attention..."

"He still would have moved," Levi finally said and then shook his head. "I loved Gavin. We grew up together, and he really was like a brother to me. But that doesn't mean he wasn't a pain in the ass."

I wanted to jump up and yell that he shouldn't say something like that, but I knew he was right.

"There's not a day that goes by that I don't think about Gavin," he continued. "And not just because of Harper or my son. I think about him because he was a part of my life for... for my whole life. I miss him every day. That's never going to change. But we all know that Gavin was... well, Gavin. He didn't like to take orders. He could be arrogant. That mission... He argued every point of it with me and with anyone who would listen."

"Yeah, but..." Declan interrupted.

"He didn't deserve to die," Levi said immediately. "He didn't deserve... to die."

"We couldn't have stopped him," Sebastian said quietly, and Declan agreed.

Levi looked directly at me. "You couldn't have stopped him, Cole. You have to know that. No one could have."

I looked at the three men who were my only family and saw it in their eyes—what Levi said was the truth. No one blamed me. No one hated me. No one thought I was a killer.

I breathed a heavy sigh of relief.

Sebastian reached over and put a hand on my shoulder before reaching for his drink with his other hand. "I think it's time we let the past stay where it belongs—in the past. It's time to start looking toward the future."

"Here, here," Declan agreed somberly, raising his glass.

Soon we each had our drinks in the air. "To Gavin," I said, and for the first time, it didn't hurt to say his name.

"To Gavin," the guys replied.

∼

It was well after midnight, and I was back in my own bed, in my own home. I couldn't sleep, and I was just staring at the ceiling. Evangeline's case was over. Part of me was relieved, but there was another part of me that—stupidly, selfishly—wished we'd had more time.

How fucked-up was that? Essentially, I was wishing for her to still be in danger.

I couldn't believe we'd all missed the signs—that Janelle had this previous connection. But then again, it was such a random and little-known fact, I could honestly say it would have been nearly impossible to find. Thousands of kids audition for those shows, and being how it was so long ago and the threats had only started recently... Well, the whole thing was bizarre.

I closed my eyes, but I could still see Evangeline's face. I didn't even fight it. I didn't even try to make the image go away. If anything, the sight of her gave me peace. For a short span of time, she needed me. Wanted me. Someone as good and clean and amazing as her actually wanted someone like me.

Why was I even here? I asked myself. Not just here on this planet, but here in this house. This town. Why would I choose to come back here? This place held nothing but negative memories. Why was I forcing myself to stay in this rut? Waiting for people to put me down and tell me I was no good?

We have something good. Something better than I've had in... ever.

Now it wasn't just her face but her voice. I played that statement over and over in my mind. I'd been with a lot of women—most of them had told me that what we had was good. But they were referring to the act, the sex, the moment. They all left and hadn't asked to come back. But Evangeline? She was referring to something more than sex, more than a moment.

And I threw that away.

Not only did I throw it away, I was cruel about it.

It didn't take a genius to realize that most of the current problems in my life were self-inflicted. I willingly moved back to a place where I knew I was going to be rejected. I'd kept everyone at a distance—even my best friends.

And I threw away the chance to finally have some peace. Some love.

A future.

And damn if I had a clue about how to change it.

Well, that wasn't true. First thing in the morning, the house goes. I'll put it on the market as-is. I didn't need the money—I made more than I needed from the security work. And then inspiration struck— Once the house sold, I'd donate the money to a women's shelter. Something like what Levi had done in his hometown for the homeless. Or better yet, I'd talk to Sebastian and the guys about maybe all of us investing in starting something like that on our own.

For my mother.

Maybe if she'd had someplace to go, a way to get out of the abusive marriage and been able to take care of herself, she wouldn't have died so young.

My chest actually felt lighter.

It was a start.

Maybe I was finally on my way to getting my shit together.

∼

It had been three weeks since I spent my last night in my childhood home. I'd been working out of our main office in DC. We each had a small space near where we lived, but being that I was up in the air with where I wanted to settle down, I was making this my home space for now.

We were looking at some potential cases along with interviewing potential guys to add to the team, and for the most part, that was keeping me busy. I put one of the case files down and scrubbed a hand over my face.

"Too much damn reading," I murmured.

Deciding I needed to refresh my coffee, I got up and went to the kitchenette. There was no one in there, but clearly there had been earlier—there were dishes in the sink and magazines scattered all over the table. I made a mental note to talk to the staff about cleaning up after themselves.

With a fresh mug in my hand, I turned to leave, but one of the magazine covers caught my eye.

Evangeline.

I knew I should have kept walking—just ignored it. But I couldn't. Placing my mug down on the table, I picked up the magazine and just took a minute to look at her. It was a current edition, and the article talked about how filming was done on the movie and how she was already generating some serious Oscar buzz for her work.

Good for her.

And I really meant it.

I watched how hard she worked and was blown away by her talent. I was proud of her. It only made sense that Hollywood would see it too. Evangeline was on the cusp of having the serious career she had always wanted and doing away with her teen-idol image.

The magazine fell from my hands as it hit me—we were no different. All the time we'd spent together, and I had mocked her, her talent, her life. She was exactly like me—trying to shake off the image that everyone had of her and becoming the person she really was and always wanted to be.

How could I have missed that? How did I not see it?

Leaving the magazine where it fell, I made my way back to my office and slammed the door. Sometimes I was my own worst enemy. I needed to do something. I needed... I just wanted... I sighed.

Her. I just wanted Evangeline.

I needed to apologize.

I needed to show her that I was wrong.

But I knew it was going to take more than a phone call. She could easily refuse my call or have someone take a message and then never call me back. No, I needed to do something more. Words were her living. Words were easy. I needed to show her—really *show* her—what she meant to me.

I sat and wracked my brain and played back every conversation we'd had when it hit me. Inspired, I turned to the computer and began to search. Leave it to Evangeline to form an attachment to something so obscure, so random, that there was only one place in the damn country you could get it.

It took longer than I thought, but I made the call and was assured it would be delivered to her on Friday. That was two days away, so I had to deal with that, but I knew it would be worth it.

And in that moment, that one exact moment where the phone call ended and I relaxed back in my chair, I felt something I had never felt before.

Hope.

And it felt really damn good.

A knock on the door a few minutes later brought me out of my reverie. "Come in."

Levi poked his head in the door. "Hey, how's it going?"

I knew he wasn't asking for any specifics, but I couldn't help but smile. "Good," I said. "What's going on?"

"Well, I know you're sort of a man without a country—so to speak—and we got an inquiry today about a potential new client."

"O-kay," I said slowly, unsure of where he was going with this.

"We've been kind of lucky that we've all been able to stay fairly local. This one takes us out of the DC, Maryland, and Virginia area. Would you be interested in checking it out?"

I shrugged. "I really don't have anything keeping me here. What kind of case is it?"

"Something that we're all looking for—some basic security. No drama. No danger. I think they may just be looking for someone to help them get something set up, but I got a feeling they might be open to hiring someone full time."

That piqued my curiosity—and my suspicion. "You trying to get rid of me?"

Levi chuckled. "Hell no. I think this could give us the perfect opportunity to branch out more. Open more offices. Who knows, eventually we could have locations all over the country."

The idea was certainly appealing. "You sure you want me to go? I'm not really the business guy. I can go in there and get a job done, but normally you or Seb go in and do the sales pitch."

"Cole," Levi said, leveling me with a stare, "you are more than capable of doing this." Then he shrugged. "Of course, if you'd rather skip a trip to New York and a weekend at the Plaza…"

"Wait, wait, wait." I interrupted. "The Plaza? Seriously?"

"Okay, maybe not the Plaza, but have you ever been to New York?"

I shook my head.

"When was the last time you even took a vacation?"

"Hell if I know..."

"Do you want to take care of this or not?" he asked with mock exasperation. "We've all taken some personal time—except you. I think you can totally handle the initial contact with these people and then take a little time for yourself."

I knew Evangeline was staying in New York right now, so maybe, just maybe, I could kill two birds with one stone. I could take care of this business and then look her up—preferably close to the time she received my gift.

I looked at Levi as I stood and extended my hand. "Done."

THIRTEEN
Evangeline

So the past few weeks should have been good.

I had some of the best publicity I'd had in my entire career—sympathy as news got out of my stalker and also genuine respect for the film. It wasn't close to being done yet, but word got out early about such things—at least when good PR people were on the job.

I should have been thrilled, overjoyed that my career was finally on the trajectory I wanted.

I wasn't.

I was having trouble thinking of anything but Cole.

It was really infuriating since he'd been an asshole and we hadn't even known each other for very long. I shouldn't feel like I'd lost everything just because he'd decided he didn't want to pursue a relationship.

But I did.

I was working on it though—looking through screenplays, having discussions with producers, focusing on what my next project should be. I had some good choices. I wasn't limited to the silly, superficial song-and-dance roles I'd been pigeonholed in before. And all the aftermath of Janelle's arrest was finally dying down. Things were really looking up.

I still desperately wanted Cole.

I was trying not to think about him on Friday afternoon as I ran hard on my treadmill. I would have preferred to box like Cole had taught me back in DC, but I hadn't thought to set up a bag here. So I was running hard and fast, sweat streaming down my face and skin under my clothes, hoping Cole was okay, that he wasn't sinking into depression, that he hadn't heard bad news when he went to hear the results of the accident that would send him into a downward spiral.

It hurt how there was nothing I could do. I didn't even know where he was.

And Sebastian had refused to give me any information. Not that I'd asked. I'd hinted, of course, but he hadn't taken the bait, and I was hating how I refused to demand an answer.

I gave a little jump when Cali came into the room, holding a package. "This was just delivered for you," she said. "Do you want me to open it for you?"

"Yeah," I huffed, slowing down just a little. I got packages fairly regularly, but they'd made me squirrely ever since I'd gotten the twisted gifts from Janelle.

The days were long gone when packages made me feel loved, like the candy my granddad used to send.

Cali put the box on the table, and I focused on running. But something struck me as familiar about the size of the package.

It was in a regular packing box, but the size looked familiar.

When she got the outer box open, I understood why.

It was a pretty pink box with silver swirl—one I'd seen many, many times before.

Inside, there would be caramels.

I jerked to a stop in my astonishment, nearly stumbling off the treadmill in my rush.

"How pretty," Cali said. "It looks like that candy you used to get." She'd been my PA since I was thirteen, so she might remember the boxes too.

My grandfather died when I was seventeen, and he'd sent them to me every week until he died.

I ran over to the table and lifted the lid of the box with shaky hands. As expected, there were two dozen wrapped caramels from the little confectioner's shop in Hillsville, Indiana, my grandparents' hometown.

It was the only place in the world you could get these particular caramels.

I stared down at them, dazed and stunned and sweaty and starting to shake with a building wave of emotion.

"There's no card," Cali said, looking through the packing box. "And nothing on the label except Hillsville Candy. Do you think these are safe? I'm not sure you should eat something you don't know where it came from."

"I know where it came from," I managed to say in a voice that didn't sound quite like me.

"Are you okay?"

I wiped away some of the sweat with my hands. Then remembered the towel hanging on a chair nearby, so I went to grab it. "Yeah. I'm okay."

"Who is this from?"

It had to be Cole. It *had* to be. He was the only person I'd ever told about how much the caramels meant to me. No one else in the world would know to buy them for me.

I'd told him they made me feel loved. Surely he would remember that. Surely he wouldn't send me these unless they meant something about his own feelings.

I was so overwhelmed with this recognition that I had to sit down abruptly since my knees were about to buckle.

Cali went to grab my water bottle from the treadmill and brought it over for me, and I drank gratefully. "So," she asked slowly, "Is this a good breakdown or a bad one? Because I'm not sure I can stand another stalker so soon."

"Not a stalker," I managed to say. "It's good."

Her face relaxed. "Oh. Good." Then she seemed to realize something. "They're from Cole, aren't they?"

I didn't answer with words, but my face must have reflected the truth.

Cali clapped her hands together. "Thank God! It's about time he manned up and did something."

I gave her a narrow-eyed look, but she just laughed it off.

Evidently, my intimidating glares weren't terribly intimidating. I'd have to take some lessons from Cole.

The idea that Cole might actually be around to give me glaring lessons make me so happy I propelled to my feet.

I wanted to see him. Now. I wanted to talk to him. I wanted to touch him, kiss him, be with him completely.

But I still didn't know where he was, and he hadn't left any sort of message.

Was he expecting me to hunt him down? Was it a gesture of affection that wasn't a promise of any sort of future?

I was in such an emotional flurry that I couldn't think of anything in the world to do. So I did the obvious thing.

I took a shower.

~

When I got out of the shower and changed in clean clothes, I came out and found Jimmy talking to Cali at my kitchen bar.

"Hi, Jimmy," I said with a smile. I was used to people showing up without warning—so I wasn't surprised to see him there, even though he hadn't called to tell me he was coming. Sometimes I wondered what it would be like to be the way other people were, to have the privacy and anonymity that most people took for granted. But losing it was part of this job, part of being a celebrity.

If I didn't like it, I could just quit.

It was nice to know that was an option if I ever decided to take it. Not yet though.

"What's going on?" I asked since he never turned up just to hang out. There was always a reason.

"Cali and I were talking," he said with a smile. "We think you need to increase your security staff."

I frowned. "What are you talking about? Is there something happening that I don't—"

"No, no." He interrupted, his smile fading. "Nothing like that. Just as a precaution."

I sighed and rubbed my face, trying to focus on this rather than on what the caramels meant, whether they meant what I thought they meant. "Okay. I guess that's fine."

Jimmy nodded and stood up. "Good. You'll want to interview anyone we hire first, right?"

"Sure. I mean, I'd like to meet them first if they're going to be lurking around me all the time to make sure I'd be comfortable with them." This whole conversation felt strange. Not at all how the normal processes worked with my hiring any sort of staff. I had no idea what was wrong with Jimmy.

"Good. I've got someone for you to interview now."

I blinked at him. "Right now?"

He nodded. "He's just outside."

I still had no idea what was happening. None at all. "Why didn't you tell me about it before?" I turned for help to Cali. "Do you know what's going on?"

She gave a little shrug, obviously hiding a smile. "I think this is a good thing."

"O-kay. Send him in, I guess."

I know it might sound crazy, but I was still completely oblivious. My mind was so distracted with other thoughts that it couldn't clearly think through exactly what was occurring right now.

Not until I saw who walked into the room.

Cole.

Not in his normal beat-up jeans and crew-neck shirt, but in trousers, a dress shirt and jacket. He still looked kind of rough, with his strong features and perpetual five o'clock shadow, but he'd obviously made a real effort.

I stared, completely dumbfounded.

"Here he is," Jimmy said, amusement in his tone. "I think he'll be a perfect fit to head up your security detail. Cali and I are going to grab some lunch. We'll talk more tomorrow."

Before I could respond or even think, both of them left, and I was alone with Cole.

His eyes were soft on my face but also questioning, a little wary.

"I don't..." I began, swallowing hard.

"I'm here about the security position."

I waved vaguely at the kitchen stool beside the one I was sitting in.

"I don't have a resume with me," he explained, his eyes never leaving mine. "But I'd like an interview just the same."

"Okay." I was starting to shake now, knowing he wouldn't be here unless the unspoken message in the caramels was true.

He felt deeply for me. He wanted me to know it for sure.

"I think I'd be good in terms of keeping you secure," he said. "I don't have a lot of experience in that kind of security work, but I want to try. For the first time in my life, I want to try."

"But you said—"

"I was scared. I didn't think I was good enough for you, for a relationship, so I just ran from everything I was feeling. But I don't want to do that anymore. I want to spend a... a long time making sure you never feel anything but secure. Possibly a lifetime."

I was gasping in response, in rising joy. "You don't want me to feel anything else?"

"Well," he said with a wry expression, "I'm hoping you'll feel some other things as well. More exciting things."

I swallowed hard. "So you're saying you want to be a... a permanent member of my security staff."

"That's right. I'm asking for no pay." He lifted his hand to cup my face. "I'll be getting plenty of benefits that will make up for that."

"What kind of benefits are you expecting to get?"

"Mainly... you."

That might have been the most romantic thing I'd ever heard in my life.

I was smiling when I replied in a lilting voice, "You don't think you should hold out for something better?"

"There is nothing better. You're the best I could ever hope for, and I know I blew it before, but I'm hoping you might give me a second chance."

I hid my face in my hands for a minute, my shoulders shaking as I suppressed the emotion. Then I lowered my hands to beam at him, because there was obviously only one answer I could voice. "Then you have the job."

He pulled me into his arms, and I felt utterly safe, utterly secure, utterly at home. No one in the world could make me feel the same way, and I felt like I was flying at the same time.

When we pulled back, his face was twisted with something that looked like regret. "I'm so sorry, Evangeline. I'm so sorry I hurt you and threw back what was so good between us as if it didn't matter. It does matter. *You* matter. More than anything to me. I'll make sure you never doubt that again."

The emotion was too strong, and I had to wipe my eyes a little, but I was barely conscious of doing so. "Thank you for the caramels."

"You deserve so much more than that."

After that, I had to kiss him. There was just no way to stop it. So a few minutes passed without anything being spoken. I was growing aroused, but my emotions were stronger, and there were more things I needed to know.

Pulling away, I perched on the stool again. "What made you change your mind?"

He shrugged and glanced away. But turned back to meet my eyes as he spoke. "It just hit home. What I was doing, over and over again. I was living out the same spiral of not feeling like I was good enough. And I was finally kind of hit over the head with how wrong that was and the kind of negative shit that happened because I was trapped by that idea."

"What negative shit?" I asked, realizing something really powerful must have happened to snap him out of it. "What happened?" Then I remembered something. "What did you hear about Gavin?"

He took a shuddering breath. "It was an accident.. I was sure it must have been me. I was so convinced of it, for no reason except I felt like that was what I deserved."

I reached out to take both his hands, thinking through what he'd said. "So no one was guilty."

"No one. Gavin made a mistake, and he paid for it unfairly. And the weird thing is the other guys thought it was them too. We were all kind of shaped by that event in different ways, and we never even talked about it."

"But you're talking now?"

"We're talking now. I want to turn over a new leaf, do things better. And the main thing I want to do better is to be the man you need." He cleared his throat. "Assuming that's what you still want."

I nearly tackled him with a hug. "I do. I really do!"

Then there was more kissing, but who could blame us. I was so happy I wanted to scream it out to anyone in the world who would listen.

Despite his gruff persona, Cole seemed to feel something similar. There was a blaze bursting out through his eyes that was absolutely breathtaking.

"I know you're still in DC and Baltimore," I said, trying to be reasonable and not just keeping hugging myself. "We'll make it work."

"Yeah, there's some good news on that front. We're trying to branch out some, and New York is the next place." He grinned. "So it's kind of convenient that you'll be here for the foreseeable future."

I gasped in surprise and relief. "Very convenient. You really are the perfect man for this job."

"I have one request," he said, reaching out to take my face again as if he couldn't quite stop himself.

"What's that?"

"If we're going to set up this... partnership, I'd really like to know your real name."

I giggled, ducking my head to hide my face in his shirt briefly. "I never tell anyone."

"Tell me."

I cleared my throat. "It's Eve."

He smiled. "Eve?"

"Eve. Not as fancy or exotic, but that's my name anyway."

"I love it," he said, his lips brushing gently against mine. "Now I get to call you Eve, when no one else in the world gets to do that."

"Well, don't call me that in front of other people. I don't want it to catch on."

"My lips are sealed."

I felt strange and exposed and also safe and respected and treasured. It was such a new combination of feelings that I could hardly process it.

"So what now?" I asked at last, feeling like everything had changed so much I couldn't even begin to process it. "I feel like we need to do something."

"Well, I had an idea." He nodded toward my bedroom with a half smile. "If you really want to do something."

I knew what he was talking about, and it was exactly what I wanted too.

"Come on," I said, grabbing his hand as I led him from the room.

When we got to the bedroom, he took my face in his hands and leaned down into another kiss, and the kiss turned into a lot more until our clothes were littering the floor.

We ended up on the bed, and our bodies moved together as we kept kissing, and both my heart and my body responded to the eager passion of his embrace.

For a long time, we drank each other in, caressing and gasping with increasing urgency. When I pushed against his shoulder, he willingly allowed me to roll us both over, letting me drape myself on top of him.

My breasts pressed into his bare chest, and my hair spilled all around us as I trailed kisses along his face, jaw, and neck.

He palmed the curve of my bottom, pushing me down into his pelvis. He felt as good as anything ever had, but I knew I wouldn't be able to take much more of this foreplay before the feel of him hard and ready against me would push me over the edge.

Cole tensed and gave an animalistic grunt in response to my squirming. "Please say you're ready for me."

I laughed against his lips. "God, yes, I'm so ready."

Cole exhaled in relief as I raised myself up and took his hard length in both my hands. I stroked it a few times, making him gasp and shift beneath me, and then he handed me a condom, which I rolled on before I lifted myself up and lowered myself over him.

We both groaned at the penetration, and then I leaned forward to claim a deep, sloppy kiss.

He rocked up beneath me, and I needed the motion, needed the friction, needed him to match my deepest rhythm.

"So good, Cole," I whispered, still pressed against him fully. "You feel so good. I missed you so much."

Then I took his earlobe between my lips. Sucked it a few times. Every time I applied suction, his pelvis bucked up involuntarily.

Letting his earlobe slip out, I murmured huskily into his ear, "Let go, Cole. Let go."

He released a long, primal growl and held my hips snugly against his as he levered us both over without pulling out.

He sank deeper inside me as I wrapped my legs around his middle, arching up with a cry of pleasure.

He pulled back and thrust—long and deep—and I responded to his motion, propelled by the need to love and be loved. Both of them at once for the first time in my life.

I gasped and rolled my hips, digging my fingers into the back of his neck. "Cole!"

He reared back and thrust again, rasping out "Eve" on the instroke.

I basked in the sound of him saying my name, my real name, one no one else ever used. Together we built up a shared motion that was urgent, hungry and almost primal in its rhythm.

I knew he was with me. That he needed this as much as I did.

"Cole!" I gasped as his hips rocked with mine.

The tension inside me broke. My body shook desperately and tightened around him as the pleasure swept through me.

Cole released a rough exclamation, freezing inside me for a moment, like he was trapped in the cusp of the moment, like he needed my help to release.

So I breathed, "Let go, my sexy protector. Let go."

And he did, the pleasure and feeling twisting on his face.

Then his arms were gathering me in, and he'd collapsed into the embrace.

It was the first time in my life I felt known for who I was, needed for who I was, loved for who I was. The first time I could give all that back.

I knew that was most important, and that Cole now knew that too. The rest of our lives, wherever they took us, could shape themselves around that one truth.

EPILOGUE
Cole

"Does this look all right?"

I turned and saw Eve standing in the doorway to our bedroom, modeling yet another outfit. "Absolutely," I said with a grin. "But then again, I thought the last four outfits looked great too. What's this all about?"

"I'm meeting the rest of your friends tonight—and their wives. I just want to make a good impression."

I could only stare. Seriously? It amazed me how this beautiful, confident woman was suddenly feeling a little self-conscious and shy. Standing, I slowly walked across the room toward her. I didn't stop until we were toe-to-toe. I put my hands on her waist and leaned my forehead against hers.

"Sweetheart, you are going to blow them all away no matter what you wear."

"Oh stop," she said softly, playfully. "I want to look nice without looking like I was trying too hard."

The chuckle came out before I could stop it. I pulled back just in time to see her pout. Reaching up, I skimmed my knuckles across her cheek. "You're beautiful," I said as I looked at her. "Absolutely perfect."

And it was the truth.

"Cole," she said shyly.

How could she not know? Slowly, gently, I let my hands cup her face so she had no choice but to look at me.

"It's the truth, Eve. Every time I look at you—and it doesn't matter if you're dressed for an event or we're sitting on the couch watching TV—you take my breath away."

Her eyes went a little wide at my admission. "Oh."

I scanned her face. It was burned in my memory, and yet I couldn't ever seem to make myself stop looking at her. "I still can't believe that someone like you could ever want someone like me."

"You underestimate yourself. I think you're pretty amazing too."

And that made me smile. She was always saying things to build up my self-confidence. Me. The man who pretty much seemed like the most confident guy in the world to outsiders, still struggled with actually feeling it. It didn't matter what she was doing—what was going on with her day—she always managed to find time to leave me a note or send me a text just to tell me she was proud of me or was thinking of me.

If it was possible, I think I actually blushed.

She started to step back. "I should probably finish getting—"

"I love you," I blurted out.

She froze. "What?"

I had no idea I was even going to say that to her, and yet now that I had, it felt good. Right. "I said... I love you." I took my own step back and looked down at my shoes. "You... you know you don't have to say it back or anything." I looked back up at her. "I just wanted you to know how I felt."

A slow smile crossed her face as she closed the distance between us. "I love you too."

It was the most natural thing in the world to pull her into my embrace and kiss her. I poured everything I felt for her into it and was rewarded with her matching me in enthusiasm. Reaching down, I began to hike up her skirt and back her up against the wall.

"Cole," she said as she felt the wall behind her. "We can't. Your friends—"

"Will completely understand," I murmured, trailing kisses along the column of her throat, loving the sounds she was making.

"No," she said and somehow managed to step away from me. "It took me a long time to find the right thing to wear, and I can't have you messing that up." She turned toward the bedroom and then gave me a sassy look over her shoulder. "But you can be damn sure I'll let you mess me up when we get home later."

Deal.

~

I thought it was going to be weird.

Actually, we all had.

Well, me, Levi, Declan, and Sebastian.

While we'd always enjoyed hanging out just the four of us, we also enjoyed just hanging out with our significant others. The thought of the eight of us going out just seemed... I don't know... strange.

The bar we chose was one that we often went to. The only difference was that now we were in one of those big booths along the perimeter of the room rather than a small table near the middle. I guess it worked out better because

Eve got recognized everywhere we went, and having a little privacy so she can enjoy her night was a definite good thing.

"Is this the first time you're out without the baby?" Kristin asked Harper.

"Kind of. We've left him with my parents and with Levi's so we can go out for dinner, but this time we're letting my parents keep him overnight." She turned and gave Levi a knowing smile. "We're looking forward to having a night to ourselves."

Levi laughed. "Don't let her fool you. We're looking forward to a good night's sleep." He took a drink of his beer. "I still can't believe he wakes up so much and how disruptive he is."

Harper elbowed him in the ribs. "Please. That's because, when it's your turn to get up, you make enough noise to wake up an army just so I'll get up and help you!"

He didn't even try to argue. "Guilty," he said with a grin and draped his arm around his wife's shoulders. "What about you guys?" he asked the group as a whole. "Who's up next for this parenthood thing?"

"Hey, don't go pushing your misery on the rest of us," Sebastian said with a laugh of his own. "Our wedding is a month away, and we want to have some time to ourselves before we even think about kids."

Ali nodded. "I've spent so many years taking care of my siblings that it's going to be nice to just have a husband to take care of."

"There's not that much of a difference," Kristin chimed in.

"Hey!" Declan declared, placing a hand over his heart as if he were wounded. "I take offense to that."

"Oh, please," she said. "I have a daughter and—"

"We," he corrected. "*We* have a daughter."

Kristin blushed. "Okay, we have a daughter. But dealing with you sometimes isn't much different than dealing with Lily."

Declan went to correct her, but we were all laughing and joking, and he soon realized that it was pointless to argue.

This was good. The laughter. The teasing. The lightness. For far too long we had all been too serious. Too focused on the past or on the complexity of cases we were working on. Which was what made me ask, "So what's next on the calendar? What is everyone going to be working on?"

Levi put his drink down. "Actually, we've got a lot of strong applicants waiting for placement. We've got a decent bunch now and a fairly full caseload. I'm thinking that—if you're all agreeable—we could quite easily step back into mentor positions. You know, not have to be working the cases directly."

"So, what? We're just sitting at desks now?" I asked. "That doesn't seem right."

Levi shrugged. "It doesn't have to be that way. But with you being based in New York now, and Harper and I staying in Virginia, and Sebastian and Ali deciding to be in DC, it just seemed like we can branch out a little. We can work on training and really get this company to branch out in ways that others haven't."

Declan cleared his throat. "I, um, I noticed you didn't mention Kristin and I during that whole thing."

"I figured you'd want to tell them," Levi said.

Looking at each of us before taking Kristin's hand, Declan said, "Actually, Kristin and I are looking at moving up to New England. Getting a fresh start with our lives. So basically, I could start up a branch up there too."

And then everyone was talking again.

"That will make it a little bit harder for us to get together for drinks," I said.

"Yeah, but I think we're all in a good place right now, and it will make the time when we actually can get together that much better," Declan said.

"Here, here," Levi and Sebastian added.

I knew it was the truth, but a part of me was a little sad. These were my friends, my brothers, my family. Ever since I had moved to New York to be with Eve, I had missed them—the time that we'd normally spend together. But it was time. Declan had the right idea. It was time for a fresh start, and maybe that all began with each of us learning to rely a little more on ourselves rather than one another.

Together we were great. Almost unstoppable.

But with the women who were now part of our lives?

We were the best.

We were home.

Placing my arm around Eve, I reached for my glass with my other hand. "I'd like to propose a toast." I waited for everyone to raise their glasses. "To the future. We've traveled a long road together—not all of it was good—but I know that I am a better man for just knowing all of you."

Before we could clink glasses, Sebastian cleared his throat. "To the business that has not only brought us financial security and success but also to the women we love."

"And to the families we now have because of them," Declan added.

As our glasses drew close, Levi stopped. "And to the man who really made all this possible." He stopped as emotion clogged his throat. "To Gavin."

"To Gavin."

ABOUT NOELLE ADAMS

Noelle handwrote her first romance novel in a spiral-bound notebook when she was twelve, and she hasn't stopped writing since. She has lived in eight different states and currently resides in Virginia, where she writes full time, reads any book she can get her hands on, and offers tribute to a very spoiled cocker spaniel.

She loves travel, art, history, and ice cream. After spending far too many years of her life in graduate school, she has decided to reorient her priorities and focus on writing contemporary romances. For more information, please check out her website: noelle-adams.com.

Books by Noelle Adams

Tea for Two Series
　　Falling for her Brother's Best Friend
　　Winning her Brother's Best Friend
　　Seducing her Brother's Best Friend

Balm in Gilead Series
　　Relinquish
　　Surrender
　　Retreat

Rothman Royals Series
　　A Princess Next Door
　　A Princess for a Bride

A Princess in Waiting
Christmas with a Prince

Preston's Mill Series (co-written with Samantha Chase)
    Roommating
    Speed Dating
    Procreating

Eden Manor Series
    One Week with her Rival
    One Week with her (Ex) Stepbrother
    One Week with her Husband
    Christmas at Eden Manor

Beaufort Brides Series
    Hired Bride
    Substitute Bride
    Accidental Bride

Heirs of Damon Series
    Seducing the Enemy
    Playing the Playboy
    Engaging the Boss
    Stripping the Billionaire

Willow Park Series
    Married for Christmas
    A Baby for Easter
    A Family for Christmas
    Reconciled for Easter
    Home for Christmas

One Night Novellas
- One Night with her Best Friend
- One Night in the Ice Storm
- One Night with her Bodyguard
- One Night with her Boss
- One Night with her Roommate
- One Night with the Best Man

Standalones
- A Negotiated Marriage
- Listed
- Bittersweet
- Missing
- Revival
- Holiday Heat
- Salvation
- Excavated
- Overexposed
- Road Tripping
- Chasing Jane
- Late Fall
- Fooling Around
- Married by Contract
- Trophy Wife
- Bay Song

ABOUT SAMANTHA CHASE

New York Times and USA Today Bestseller/contemporary romance writer Samantha Chase released her debut novel, Jordan's Return, in November 2011. Although she waited until she was in her 40's to publish for the first time, writing has been a lifelong passion. Her motivation to take that step was her students: teaching creative writing to elementary age students all the way up through high school and encouraging those students to follow their writing dreams gave Samantha the confidence to take that step as well.

When she's not working on a new story, she spends her time reading contemporary romances, blogging, playing way too many games of Scrabble on Facebook and spending time with her husband of 25 years and their two sons in North Carolina. For more information visit her website at www.chasing-romance.com.

Books by Samantha Chase

Jordan's Return
The Christmas Cottage
Ever After
Catering to the CEO
In the Eye of the Storm
Wait for Me
Trust in Me
Stay With Me
A Touch of Heaven
Mistletoe Between Friends
The Snowflake Inn
The Baby Arrangement
Baby, I'm Yours

Baby, Be Mine
Exclusive
Moonlight in Winter Park
Duty Bound
Honor Bound
Forever Bound
Home Bound
The Wedding Season
Return to You
Meant for You
I'll Be There
Made for Us
Live, Love & Babies Trilogy
Love Walks In
Christmas in Silver Bell Falls
Waiting for Midnight
Always My Girl

Website: www.chasing-romance.com
Facebook: www.facebook.com/SamanthaChaseFanClub
Twitter: https://twitter.com/SamanthaChase3
Pinterest: http://www.pinterest.com/samanthachase31/

Made in the USA
Columbia, SC
11 July 2020

12869675R00136